FAST AND DANGEROUS

Frank could see a black sport-utility vehicle trailing them. "Lose him, Joe," he said, his jaw tight.

"Right." Joe turned the van quickly. After a few miles, the street was clear behind them. Joe pulled the van to a stop on a dark, deserted street in front of a long row of waterfront warehouses.

"That was some ride. Your Indy track experience is showing," Frank said.

"Yeah, yeah," Joe quipped. "Well, I got the job done, didn't I?"

Just as Frank was about to answer, he was jolted out of his seat and sent sprawling on the van floor. Something had slammed into the rear of the van like a ton of bricks. Frank and Joe were about to be crushed.

Nancy Drew & Hardy Boys SuperMysteries

Available from ARCHWAY Paperbacks

A NANCY AND HARDY DREW AND BOYS SUPER MYSTERY™

OUT OF CONTROL

Carolyn Keene

AN ARCHWAY PAPERBACK
Published by POCKET BOOKS
New York London Toronto Sydney Tokyo Singapore

AN ARCHWAY PAPERBACK *Original*

An Archway Paperback published by
POCKET BOOKS, a division of Simon & Schuster Inc.
1230 Avenue of the Americas, New York, NY 10020

Copyright © 1997 by Simon & Schuster Inc.
Produced by Mega-Books, Inc.

ISBN: 0-671-53748-2

First Archway Paperback printing June 1997

10 9 8 7 6 5 4 3 2 1

NANCY DREW, THE HARDY BOYS, AN ARCHWAY PAPERBACK and colophon are registered trademarks of Simon & Schuster Inc.

A NANCY DREW AND HARDY BOYS SUPERMYSTERY is a trademark of Simon & Schuster Inc.

Cover art by Franco Accornero

Printed in the U.S.A.

IL 6+

OUT OF CONTROL

Chapter

One

MAN, I NEVER GET tired of that sound," seventeen-year-old Joe Hardy said as a race car roared around the first turn and into the short chute of the Indy 500 track of the Indianapolis Motor Speedway.

The car disappeared into the back straightaway at 231 miles per hour, and Joe jumped up to watch it, aching to be inside the car.

"As far as locations go, this is going to be one of the best cases we've been on," Frank Hardy said with a grin. Frank was a year older than his brother and an inch taller, with dark brown hair and eyes. He shared blond-haired Joe's love of automobile racing.

"Undercover on Robbie MacDonnell's crew.

1

A-*ma*-zing," Joe said, shaking his head. "Speaking of the case, has Mr. Brandon called yet?"

"Nope," Frank said. "He must still be in Scotland. He sure is a low-profile client—I've only seen him once. But he's supposed to be back here for qualifications this Saturday."

Joe thought for a moment. He knew that qualifications were the official lead-up to the Indianapolis 500. The thirty-three drivers with the fastest times would be eligible for the big race. "Mr. Brandon wants to make sure the car he spent a million dollars on qualifies for the race," Joe pointed out. "Think this team will be ready?"

"We'd better be," Frank said.

The Hardys were standing in the Team Brandon pit, taking a break from working on Robbie's backup car. Robbie MacDonnell, the hotshot Scottish race driver, was only twenty-two, but he had burned up the European circuit and was ready for the Indianapolis 500. Unfortunately, his car and team had been plagued by mechanical glitches and strange occurrences since they had arrived in Indianapolis.

The team owner, Duncan Brandon, another Scotsman, had hired the Hardys to investigate the occurrences to rule out sabotage. Now the boys were working undercover as part of the mechanics' crew.

Joe had some experience racing a stock car, and both Hardys knew enough about cars to pass as mechanics without arousing the suspicions of the rest of the crew.

"It's Thursday, and quals are day after tomorrow," Frank said. "I'd like to have some answers for Mr. Brandon when he gets here."

"In the meantime," Joe said, "let's enjoy every moment we've got." He glanced around, taking in the scene. Above him, two team members stood in the team timer box, a small platform perched a few yards above the ground with a good view of the track. With computerized timers, they clocked the speeds of Robbie's competitors doing practice runs.

A high chain-link fence separated the rear of the pit from the spectators' seats. At the front, a low structure, called the pit wall, ran along the edge of the two-and-a-half-mile oval track. On race day, drivers would streak around the track two hundred times to the finish. Along the straightaway, the long side of the oval, they'd often go over 240 miles per hour.

"Okay, here's what we know so far," Joe said, leaning against the pit wall. Both Hardys were dressed in the yellow jumpsuits and caps of Robbie's team, mechanics' badges clipped to their waists. "The burned piston was legitimate—nothing sneaky, right?"

"Right. But the damaged undertray and

turbocharger were probably sabotage. I don't know how we could ever prove it, though."

"And our chief suspect is Giovanni Randisi," Joe said.

"He's got the best motive," Frank said, nodding. "He was fired from Robbie's crew because he was suspected of stealing parts. Maybe he's looking for a little revenge.

"Plus, he's working for Jean-Claude Rochefort now," Joe pointed out.

"Who happens to be Robbie's chief rival for Rookie of the Year," Frank added.

"Right, and Randisi still has access to the garage area."

"But the biggest problem they've had so far is Sandy MacDonnell's absence," Frank said. "You don't suppose something's happened to him, do you?"

"Maybe," Joe replied. "He's Robbie's brother and chief mechanic, and he's not here the week before qualifications. Something's definitely wrong."

"Did you get a chance to talk to Robbie about him this morning?"

"Yep," Frank said. "He mentioned that Sandy had left a note saying he had a personal emergency in Chicago and he'd be here today—but there's no sign of him yet. I asked Robbie if he'd talked to Sandy at all. He said no, but he didn't seem to be too upset about it. He said that his brother will show up and that Jay's our chief until then."

"I talked to the crew members I was working with this morning," Joe reported. "None of them has a clue where Sandy is. One guy tried to locate him but came up empty."

"Well, maybe Mr. Brandon will have some ideas."

Joe hoisted himself onto the pit wall and peered up the track. It was a clear sunny day, so the stands were half full of spectators. The stands held more than 300,000 people, and on race day another 100,000 to 150,000 would jam the infield.

Joe heard a piercing squeal as a car pushed out of the groove in the fourth turn. It spun a couple of times as it passed the Hardys, then headed for the first turn.

"Sandy's crazy," Joe said, his heart pounding. "Why would he want to be in Chicago when he could be here?"

"I wish we could stay in Indianapolis for more than ten days," Nancy Drew said to her friend George Fayne. Eighteen-year-old Nancy pushed her reddish blond hair back from her face as she read. "This brochure is packed with things to do."

It was the end of May—Indy 500 Festival month in Indianapolis—and Nancy and George were in town for the celebration.

"We missed the queen's ball and the drivers' softball game," Nancy said as she read, "but we can take in the sports art exhibition, the mini-marathon, the parade, and tons of concerts and parties."

"First on my list is Indy 500 qualifications this weekend," George said. "Second is the Indy 500 itself, a week from Sunday." Dark-haired George was an avid sports participant and fan, with the lean body of an athlete. "What's scheduled for today?" she added.

Nancy scanned the pull-out calendar from the brochure. "Thursday, one o'clock," she read. "Kate Cordova is previewing a fashion show. The public is invited."

"Kate Cordova?"

"Oh, you know, that young designer. She's only twenty-four. They're going to do a runway show and some magazine layouts featuring Miranda Marott."

"The teen supermodel?" George said with a barely stifled yawn. "A fashion show, hmm?"

"Actually, the show's the night before the race. They're doing a shoot today for a magazine layout." She grinned at George. "It's at Gasoline Alley at the track."

George's expression brightened. "The track?

What are we waiting for? Let's go." She grabbed her bag and headed for the door.

Nancy tucked in her blue T-shirt, tied a white sweater around her waist, and grabbed her keys.

Downstairs at the Barbary Inn Bed and Breakfast, Alice Froman, the innkeeper, waved goodbye as they climbed into Nancy's blue Mustang.

Nancy drove down the hill that led into the tunnel under the Indy 500 track. A race car streaked over their heads, and Nancy felt the roar rumble through her stomach.

Her face flushed with excitement as they came out of the tunnel and into the infield, a lush green golf course during the rest of the year. Race cars zoomed 360 degrees around them.

Spectators and tourists wandered through the infield and in and out of the sparkling white limestone Hall of Fame museum and other attractions. Nancy parked the car in a lot before she and George walked over to a large fenced area at one end of the track. A sign above the entrance proclaimed it to be Gasoline Alley, which led from the garages out to the track. A guard in a bright yellow shirt stood at the entrance next to the open gate.

Next to him, a tour guide announced, "Although special passes are usually needed to get into the garage area, we are going to let a limited number of you through the gate this afternoon. Miss Cordova wants tourists in the background of the fashion photos that are being taken before the show. Those of you in the front, follow me, please."

Nancy and George stepped quickly through the gate. They were led over to a small area enclosed by a thick red rope. The tour guide sat in a chair off to one side as the onlookers crowded together.

Nancy and George stood in the front of the group. Six attractive teen models, dressed in outdoor activewear, were having their hair and makeup done.

"Which one's Miranda Marott?" George asked.

"I don't see her yet," Nancy said. "Besides, I'm busy watching them." She nodded to a half-dozen young men standing nearby. A couple were dressed in drivers' jumpsuits, the others in jeans and shirts. They were all good-looking and in their twenties.

"Now you're talking," George said. "Drivers! Look—there's Bobby Purdy from California and Jean-Claude Rochefort from Monaco. I think that's Italy's John Macri in the purple jumpsuit."

A pink- and orange-striped trailer, with Be a Sport!—Kate Cordova Designs painted on the side, anchored the scene on the right. Ahead, a black curtain was strung between two towering lightposts, making a thirty-foot-by-thirty-foot backdrop.

A tall stepladder stood in front of the curtain next to a ten-foot pedestal. A crane truck drove into view with a huge silver urn hanging from its hook. "That looks like the 500 trophy," Nancy said.

"It is," the tour guide said. "Sterling silver, four feet, four inches tall, ninety-two pounds. There's a three-dimensional sculpted bust of each of the Indy 500 winners around the sides of the trophy. It stands in Victory Lane during May. The rest of the year, it's in the museum."

"Big mistake, hauling that trophy here," a guard muttered. "I'd feel a lot better if they'd left it on the pedestal that was made for it, not that tall thing they rigged up here. I just hope they made the pedestal sturdy enough. If the trophy fell, it could kill someone."

"Call Miranda!" A woman's voice thundered through a megaphone as the crane hoisted the huge trophy up onto the ten-foot pedestal. Two men scrambled up the stepladder to help position it.

"There she is," Nancy said. The crowd buzzed with recognition as the world's leading teen supermodel, Miranda Marott, approached them. She wore sleek black bicycle shorts and a red-striped tank top. Her long pale blond hair was pulled high in a shiny ponytail. She cautiously climbed each rung of the ladder until she sat on top next to the trophy.

When Miranda was seated, the photographer called to her. "Okay, Miranda, now I want you to kiss the trophy."

A man carrying a large spotlight crouched at the foot of the pedestal and aimed a pink light up at Miranda. The model pursed her lips and leaned toward the trophy.

As Nancy watched, a ripple in the backdrop curtain caught her eye. Something's not right, she told herself.

Nancy looked up, straining to see against the pink light. A sudden streak of horror shot down her spine as she saw the huge trophy tremble, then begin to topple. The man with the spotlight was directly under it, and it was headed straight toward him like a huge silver bomb.

Chapter

Two

"THE TROPHY!" Nancy yelled as she ducked under the red rope that held back the on-lookers.

She dove toward the lighting man, who seemed unable to move as the trophy plunged straight down at him.

Nancy tackled him, moving him away from danger as the trophy hit the ground. Nancy felt bits of gravel pelt the back of her head.

The man glanced over at Nancy, and a rosy flush spread across his forehead. His dark blue eyes were wide with shock, and his chest pumped as he gasped for air.

"Whew!" he said in a rush of outgoing breath. "That was close. Thanks!"

"It's okay." Nancy nodded. She glanced over at the trophy. It was still intact.

"What happened?" the man asked as Nancy let go of his arm.

"I'm not sure," she replied. "I was watching Miranda when I saw the trophy start to wobble—"

"Jason! Are you okay?" Nancy was interrupted by a young woman who swept through the crowd of onlookers. Her black hair was cropped very short, and she was dressed in black leggings and a flowing black shirt. "Get out of my way!" she commanded as she approached.

As two guards from the museum checked the trophy, a third man tried to hold back the crowd pushing against the high fence.

"I'm okay, Kate," the man said. "Thanks to her," he added, nodding to Nancy.

The woman smiled at Nancy. "I'm Kate Cordova."

"I'm Nancy Drew."

Taking advantage of the accident, the large crowd spilled past the guards into Gasoline Alley and surrounded the trophy and the famous designer. Television crews jammed microphones between Nancy and Kate. The designer grinned at the cameras and gave quick answers to all the questions.

Finally, Kate turned to Nancy, saying with a shudder, "Thanks for saving my assistant from being flattened by that ton of silver. This is Jason Randell."

Nancy could see the affection and worry in Kate's dark brown eyes. "I couldn't do my job without Jason," the young designer concluded.

Jason turned away from the cameras, flashed a quick, nervous smile at Nancy, then ducked into the crowd.

"That's all," Kate said to the reporters. "An accident. It's over. No one's hurt. No more story."

The man who had worked on the models' hair pushed through.

"Where's Miranda?" he asked.

"I don't know," Kate answered. "Probably in the trailer, sulking."

The stylist rolled his eyes and headed toward the pink-and-orange trailer. Kate reached into her pocket and pulled out a business card and pen to scribble a note. Then she handed the card to Nancy and sputtered a few words as she began running after Jason. "Thanks again. Come to supper, my loft . . . bring friends."

Nancy read the note on the back of the card: "12th floor, 8 tonight, casual."

As the crowd calmed a little, a half-dozen Indy 500 guards herded it toward the gate leading out of Gasoline Alley. More guards, with the help of a few city police and the crane, had placed the trophy on a truck to be taken to the silversmith to be checked for damage.

Figuring George would wait for her, Nancy slipped away from the crowd and stepped behind the pedestal. What had made the trophy topple? she wondered. What—or who—had moved the curtain just before the trophy had fallen?

She pulled back the edge of the curtain and peered into a large space. The curtain had been strung across the open door of one of the garages in Gasoline Alley. The room was dark—a perfect place for someone to hide.

Nancy slipped behind the curtain and squinted her eyes to adjust to the dimness. Mechanics' tools and other equipment were scattered around, including a few long poles, a block-and-tackle rigging, and a couple of stepladders and stools.

"Hey!"

Nancy gasped at the sudden sound of the deep voice behind her. A chill rippled across her shoulders as light filled the garage. She turned quickly to face a large man in a police uniform.

"I've been looking for you," he said. "You're the gal who pushed that guy out of the way, aren't you? What are you doing in here?"

Nancy smiled broadly. "I just wanted to look around. I've never been to the track before."

"I suggest you take an official tour, miss. If you'll come with me, please, my partner and I would like to ask you a few questions."

Nancy followed the officer outside to a squad car. Leaning against the side was a short woman, whom he introduced as Detective Grace Cook. "And I'm Officer Brantley Washington, miss. Now, if you'll tell us who you are and what happened before the trophy fell, please."

Detective Cook wrote in a small notebook as Nancy identified herself and told them what she had seen.

Finally, the two officers asked where she could be reached. After Nancy gave them the information, Officer Washington walked her to the gate where George was waiting. "Here's my card," he said. "If you can think of anything more, Miss Drew, please give me a call."

As they walked back to her car, Nancy told George about the scene behind the curtain. Then she handed Kate's card to George. "I almost forgot, George. We've been invited to a party."

"I thought Robbie was taking the backup car out for a few laps," Frank said. "And speaking of laps, there goes Jean-Claude Rochefort." Frank checked his watch and shook his head.

Jean-Claude's doing two twenty-four on the straightaway. Where's Robbie? There's not that much practice time left."

Joe looked up Pit Row. "I haven't seen him for a while, either."

"Maybe he's back in the garage."

"I'll find him," Joe offered. "He'd better get that baby on the track."

Joe left the pits and walked down the ramp to Gasoline Alley. A guard checked Joe's ID as he walked through the gate into the restricted area. Joe glanced at the crowd at the far end of the garage area. A beautiful girl was climbing a ladder next to the 500 trophy.

"What's going on?" Joe asked the guard.

"They're taking pictures for some fashion thing," the guard answered, shaking his head. "I don't like it. Too many civilians running around, if you ask me. Can't keep track of them all."

Joe checked his watch, then hurried to the Team Brandon garage. Robbie was inside, taking his racing uniform out of a locker. "Hey, I thought you wanted to shake down the backup car," Joe said. "You'd better hustle."

"I'm coming, I'm coming," Robbie said, climbing into the uniform.

"What's it like out there?" Joe asked. "I've raced stock cars, but I've never been in an Indy car."

"Yeah, I've heard you're quite a throttle jockey," Robbie said, flashing a huge smile of snowy white teeth. He was about Joe's size, with a mop of wavy dark red hair and a fair complexion. "Fast speeds don't scare you, do they? How'd you like to try driving a real race car?"

"You're kidding! I'd give *anything!*"

Robbie closed the door and locked it. Then he unzipped his shiny white jumpsuit with the bright yellow stripe across the chest. "Come on," he said, throwing Joe the jumpsuit. "Strip down and put this on."

His heart thumping, Joe peeled off his jacket, T-shirt, and jeans, and slipped on the white flame-retardant knit undersuit. It felt similar to thermal underwear.

Then Robbie handed Joe a remote radio earphone, which Joe anchored in his right ear. Next, Joe pulled on the one-piece flame-retardant knit headgear. It reminded him of a ski mask with only two openings for his eyes.

"This is going to work," Robbie said, chuckling, as Joe stepped into the jumpsuit and fastened the cuffs at his ankles and wrists. "We're the same size and build, and the only part of you that anyone will see is your eyes. They're blue like mine. I know we can pull this off."

"Wait a minute. You mean I'm going to

pretend I'm you?" Joe looked at Robbie in surprise. "That's against the track rules."

"You won't be able to go on the track otherwise."

Joe hesitated for a split second, but the lure of the track was too much. It was a once-in-a-lifetime chance. He snapped on the white-and-yellow crash helmet and pulled on Robbie's white racing gloves.

"Now, listen carefully," Robbie said. "You can't talk to anyone."

Joe nodded. He was starting to swelter and itch in the multilayered uniform.

"When you get to the pit, just hop in the car. I'm usually so focused I don't talk much before a ride. People see what they want to see, Joe. They're expecting me, and they'll be convinced that's who they're looking at." Robbie put on Joe's jumpsuit and cap, tugging on the bill so that it hid his face.

"Take it around for a warm-up lap or two," he continued, "but only up to one hundred fifty or one hundred sixty miles per hour. You don't want to get carried away your first time out. If you stay at that speed, it'll look like there's something wrong with the car, and the crew will wave you off the course early." He showed Joe the speaker for the remote radio. "Don't worry. I'll talk you through it."

"But what happens when I get back to the pit? The crew will expect me—you—to tell them what's wrong with the car."

"Hmmm." Robbie thought for a minute, then grinned. "When you get out of the car, refuse to speak to anyone. Act like you're angry about the car. Brush everybody off and storm back here. I'll meet you, and we'll switch uniforms."

Joe's mind raced. He was sure Robbie was right—it could work. Robbie was well known as a hothead, so storming away from the pits would be right in character. Still, Joe hesitated. "Where are you going to be while I'm out there?" he asked.

"On the ramp leading to the pits. They'll be watching you and won't even notice me. Let's go."

A shiver of excitement rippled down Joe's spine as he realized he was only minutes away from driving around the legendary track.

Joe and Robbie left the garage, walking quickly through Gasoline Alley to the track and the MacDonnell pit. Robbie stopped at the ramp, tucking himself back into the shadows of the stands where he wouldn't be noticed.

His heart pounding with anticipation, Joe walked to Robbie's race car. The team was checking the tires and adding fuel. Frank greeted him with a smile, saying, "You barely made it, man. We're down to the last half hour of practice."

Joe avoided Frank's gaze and walked straight to the car. He wriggled his slim, muscular body down into the cockpit. A crew member squinted as he strapped Joe in and placed the earphones over his head. Joe thought his cover was blown. Did the mechanic recognize him?

The moment passed, and the mechanic moved away. Joe felt the roar of the powerful engine vibrating through his body. He heard a hard slap on the rear of the car, the signal that his qualification ride was a go.

With a quick press on the gas, Joe zoomed away from the pits. In seconds, he reached the exit from Pit Row and was out on the track. He could hear Robbie's voice in his ear, easing him along.

The cheers of a hundred thousand people resounded through his tight helmet. Their faces were blurry as he steadily increased speed.

"Remember, Joe," Robbie said in his ear, "One-sixty! Don't let it out any more than that. The crew will flag you back in when they think you can't get it any faster. Enjoy, old buddy!"

Joe settled into the dark groove on the track, curled through the second turn, and zoomed into the straightaway at 110 miles an hour. His heart racing like a turbo, he gently pressed on the gas. The car was so light, he felt as if he were flying toward the fourth turn.

Suddenly, he felt a yank on his shoulder as the car pulled sharply to the right.

"Whoa! What was that?"

"What is it, Joe?" Robbie's voice filled his ear. "What happened?"

"I—I don't know . . . it's pulling!"

"Bring it in!" Robbie radioed. "Slow it down and bring it in. You'll be at the Pit Row entrance in seconds."

The urgency in Robbie's voice added to the tension as Joe wrestled with the wheel to correct the race car's sharp pull to the right. He lifted off the throttle and eased on the brakes. Just then he felt a snap in the rear of the car. His stomach lurched as the car vaulted at 116 miles an hour toward the fourth-turn wall. He braced himself for the impact.

Chapter
Three

"Joe! Don't panic!" Robbie commanded him as Joe saw the fourth-turn wall dead ahead.

With one last frantic effort, he spun the car to the left. It leaped across the track and into the infield, grazing the pit wall as it plunged forward. After several dizzying spins in the grass, the powerful machine came to rest.

Joe unstrapped himself and shimmied slowly up and out of the car. An emergency vehicle sped across the infield to Joe's car. A tow truck followed with three crew members from the Brandon team.

As Joe took a few hesitant steps, Frank jumped off the tow truck and ran over to him. When Joe lifted his helmet and peeled off his protective knit headpiece, Frank stopped short, gaping in disbelief.

"I ought to wring your neck!" he said to Joe. "This is the worst stunt you've ever pulled!"

"Hey, it was Robbie's idea."

Frank shook his head. The fire crew ran up with fire extinguishers.

"I don't need those," Joe told them. "I'm fine." The crew looked startled when they saw Joe's face, then nodded and began to examine the damaged car.

"Are you sure?" Frank asked his brother.

Joe smiled sheepishly. "Yeah, I'm okay."

Another rescue car pulled up, and Robbie—still dressed in Joe's mechanic's jumpsuit—jumped out of the driver's seat. He ran straight to Joe.

"What happened?" Robbie asked.

"I'm not sure. Something broke. I felt a snap in the rear, and the car shimmied out."

"Looks like it was the suspension rod, Robbie," a mechanic said as the rear of the car was lifted by the tow hook.

Joe and Robbie rode on the front fenders of the tow truck as it pulled the race car back down Pit Row past the crowd. Joe knew they must realize he was not Robbie MacDonnell.

When they got to the garage, an angry Speedway official was waiting. Robbie led him into the garage and shut the door while Joe, Frank, and the others waited outside.

After a short silence, Robbie's voice boomed out from behind the garage door. An equally angry official countered with a few choice phrases. Finally, both men emerged. The official's expression was grim and determined. Robbie had changed out of Joe's mechanic's jumpsuit, and his face was a vivid red.

The official stalked off without a word. "It's bad," Robbie said, "but it could have been worse. I talked them out of suspending me from the race, but I'm getting hit with a twenty-five-thousand-dollar fine. The official wanted you off the crew, Joe, but I talked him out of that, too."

Robbie tossed Joe's jeans and jacket at him. "I told him it was my fault, but just to be on the safe side, you'd better stay out of everybody's way for a while. Get changed, and you and Frank take a lunch break. We'll see you back here in a couple of hours."

Joe darted into the garage and slipped out of the jumpsuit and into his jeans and T-shirt. When he came back outside, the rest of the crew had gathered. No one said a word, but several crew members scowled at Joe.

As they headed out of Gasoline Alley, they heard a familiar voice calling to them. "Frank and Joe Hardy!"

The Hardys turned toward the gate, where they saw their old friends Nancy and George. "I don't believe it!" Frank yelled. "What are you doing here?" he asked Nancy.

"We're tourists," Nancy said. "We came out to watch a fashion shoot. How about you? Are you here for the race?"

"Well—" Joe began with a crooked grin.

"Wait a minute," Nancy said, turning to Joe. "We just heard that some hotshot hijacked a car and took it for a spin. That was you, right?"

"Yeah, that was me," Joe answered. "And believe it or not, I wish I hadn't done it."

"You're not hurt?" George asked.

"Just his pride," Frank said with a grin. "But he'll get over that in no time. We're about to get something to eat. Want to join us?"

"Sure," Nancy answered. "We can take my car. I'm parked right over there."

Over pizza at the Straightaway, Nancy and George told the Hardys about the fashion shoot and the trophy accident.

"That must have been the crowd I saw when I came out of the garage with Robbie," Joe commented.

"Robbie?" George said. "Do you mean Robbie MacDonnell?"

"The one and only—by far the best rookie in the field," Joe said.

"He's hot stuff," George said with a smile.

Nancy had heard that Robbie was very attractive and had quite a reputation as a charmer as well as a race driver.

Frank and Joe told Nancy and George about being hired by Duncan Brandon to investigate the suspicious incidents plaguing his racing team.

"Has anything happened since you came on board?" Nancy asked.

Joe swigged his cola and thought for a moment. "It looks like my accident may have been caused by a broken suspension rod," he answered. "I'll check it later for signs of sabotage. Besides that, Robbie's brother, the chief mechanic, hasn't been here for the past week. That's pretty weird."

Frank told them why Sandy's disappearance was upsetting. "The drivers and the teams work and practice all May, but this week is the most important time of the month. Qualifying the car is everything. If the car doesn't get in, it's all over for the team for this year's race."

"You take practice runs every day this week, testing the car. Then you bring it back to the garage and work on it some more—always trying to make it faster and more efficient," Joe explained. "The chief mechanic is the most important man on the team—next to the driver, of course."

"Sandy's supposed to arrive today," Frank said, "but no one's seen him yet."

"Maybe he'll show up this afternoon," George said. "It's still early."

"He'd better," Joe muttered.

"Speaking of this evening, we've been invited to supper at Kate Cordova's tonight, and she said to bring friends," Nancy told the Hardys. "You guys qualify. Want to come? There'll be lots of pretty teen models."

"Sounds like my kind of party," Joe said, grinning, "but we have to pass."

"Yeah," Frank said. "We have to work on the car he nearly wrecked."

"I'm only on till six, remember?" Joe said. "Then it's carbo-load time at Union Station."

"Joe is running in the minimarathon tomorrow morning," Frank explained to Nancy and George. "It's the largest thirteen-point-one-mile race in the country—sixteen thousand runners, walkers, and wheelchair racers."

"It's cool," Joe added. "Halfway through the race, we take a turn around the Indy track."

"The racers get a big pasta dinner tonight," Frank said. He grabbed the bill and motioned to the waitress. "We have tomorrow morning off, so why don't we pick you up at seven, and the three of us will watch Joe tackle Killer Hill?"

"Sounds great," Nancy said as George nodded. Nancy gave Frank their address and phone number before driving the Hardys back to the track.

Robbie's crew members were more relaxed when the Hardys returned.

Jay Ronald, who was serving as chief mechanic in Sandy's absence, scowled at Joe, then punched him lightly in the shoulder, saying, "So, you thought you'd take a spin around the track."

"Cool it, Jay," Robbie said from the corner of the garage. "I told you it was my idea."

"Joe just went along for the ride, right?" Jay said with a chuckle. "Okay, Hardy, you can stay. Lucky for you, the backup can be fixed."

"It was definitely the suspension rod," Robbie explained. "It failed, and that's why you lost control."

Joe shuddered when he remembered his ride. He knew the suspension rod was part of the system that connected the wheel axles to the chassis. He was lucky one of the tires hadn't spun off the car.

"The main problem we have now comes from when you kissed the pit wall," Jay added. "We have to rebuild the chassis. I want you to keep tearing down the engine while the rest of us grab something to eat."

Joe checked his watch. "Okay, but I've only

got a few hours. I'm out of here at six, remember?"

"Yeah, yeah, I remember."

The rest of the crew took off, and Frank and Joe picked up where they had left off, systematically dismantling the car Joe had driven.

Robbie watched for a few minutes, then checked the refrigerator. "We're out of sodas. Hold down the fort—I'll get some for us."

"You know, it's a miracle you didn't kill yourself," Frank said after Robbie had left. He reached down and lifted the steering assembly out of the race car's pod.

"Yeah," Joe answered, his voice low. "I know." He pulled the broken suspension rod out of a packing crate and examined it, looking for signs of sabotage. "Frank?" he called from the corner of the garage. "Come here and take a look at this."

Frank walked over to where Joe stood by the packing boxes.

"Does this look like it might have been cut?" Joe asked.

"I don't know." Frank took the rod from Joe and turned it over in his hand. "Yeah, it does—especially here." He ran his thumb over the end. Part of it was broken and jagged, part smooth. "It's hard to tell for sure."

Joe felt a gut-grinding surge. "If so, it means that—"

"It definitely was no accident," Frank concluded. "Man, we've got to find out what's happening around here."

"If someone did cut this rod," Joe said, taking it back from Frank, "he had to have access to Gasoline Alley."

"And maybe even this garage."

"Come to think of it, how come no one mentioned this?" Joe said as he held up the broken piece. "Whoever dismantled and packed this rod must have noticed it."

"Not necessarily. They're looking for mechanical glitches; we're looking for something suspicious."

"Or the person who removed this part might have known that it was cut and packed it away so no one could give it a close inspection." Joe frowned. "It was in one of the crates with scrap material."

"Then you think someone on Robbie's crew is responsible for the sabotage?" Frank asked.

Before Joe could answer they were interrupted by a commotion outside the door. "Wrap the rod up carefully," Frank said. "Then stash it in your bag and take it with you when you leave. I'll see what's going on."

Frank moved quickly to the door. Outside, someone was yelling at Robbie, and a small crowd had gathered to watch.

"Look, Rochefort," Robbie finally said, "it's

not really any of your concern. It's a private matter between me and the track. Just run along and attend to your own business. Get in some extra practice laps—I hear you'll need them."

Frank recognized the other man as Jean-Claude Rochefort, the racer from Monte Carlo. He looked like his publicity photos—well groomed, with sleek dark hair and rugged good looks.

When Joe appeared in the doorway, the man who was yelling at Robbie whipped around and focused on Joe.

"And you," Rochefort yelled. "You'll pay, too. I'll see to that."

"Hey, man," Joe said. "Easy. I don't know what you're talking about."

"I'm talking about that little stunt you and MacDonnell pulled out on the track," Rochefort said. He turned back to Robbie. "How could you let a crew member drive your car, pretending he was you?"

"Calm yourself, Jean-Claude," Robbie said, putting a reassuring hand on Rochefort's shoulder. "I've been punished for it. I'm sure you heard about the fine, and if it happens again, I'm out of the race—so I won't be pulling any more pranks, believe me."

Jean-Claude shoved Robbie's hand away. "Don't touch me!" he yelled. "Yes, I heard about your puny little penalty. It's not nearly enough. That's why my team and I have filed a formal protest against you and Team Brandon."

"Why, you—" Robbie took a step toward Rochefort, but the other driver held his ground.

"We are going to insist that they penalize you further," Rochefort said. "In fact, we say you should be suspended from the race."

Frank and Joe watched Robbie's face redden. "Look, you miserable little worm," Robbie said through clenched teeth. "You're just trying to get me out because you haven't a chance of winning this race otherwise. You're a loser— and everyone knows it."

"Those are pretty strange words coming from a man whose own chief mechanic can't be bothered to show up during qualification week," Rochefort said with a sneer.

"Take that back, you rotten—" Without finishing his thought, Robbie lunged at Rochefort and landed a solid punch on the man's jaw.

Rochefort swung back, but Robbie ducked, and the punch missed. Rochefort lost his balance and stumbled into the garage wall.

"Easy," Frank said, putting his hand on Robbie's arm. "Don't let him bait you."

Robbie started forward, then stopped. "You're right. He's definitely not worth it."

Rochefort rubbed his jaw, his eyes narrowing.

"No point in fighting here, is there? I'll save my retaliation for where it really counts. You'll *never* race at Indy—I'll see to that!"

Rochefort's mouth widened slightly into a nasty smile. In a low, steady voice he murmured, "In fact . . . you may never race again."

Chapter

Four

THAT DOES IT!" Robbie yelled. "Let go of me, Frank. I'm going to smash that weasel's face right into the cement."

Frank held tightly to Robbie's arm, and Rochefort didn't blink.

"Remember what you told me," Frank said softly to Robbie. "He's not worth it."

Robbie shook off Frank's hand and wheeled around to face Frank and Joe. He said, "I don't want him or any of his team near our garage, do you understand?

"All right," Robbie finally muttered. "Let's get back to work on that engine. Check everything again." Then he stormed off toward the track.

Led by Jay Ronald, the rest of the crew had wandered back in during Robbie's last speech. They took off for the Brandon garage now. The Hardys lingered until they were out of earshot. Joe said in an excited whisper, "Maybe it's not Randisi causing all the trouble. Maybe it's his driver, Jean-Claude Rochefort."

"Or both," Frank said.

"If we can just get some proof," Joe muttered, and he followed Frank back to the garage.

At eight-fifteen that evening, Nancy and George were on the street where Kate Cordova's loft was. The night air was cool, and the girls were dressed in sweaters and jeans. Driving slowly, Nancy scanned the buildings. "Let's get out and look for Kate's building," she suggested. "It's in a converted factory somewhere near here."

Nancy parked under one of the pink-blossomed crab apple trees that lined the narrow, winding street. Then she and George climbed out and made their way past art galleries, coffeehouses, and music clubs until they found Kate's building.

In a cavernous freight-size elevator, Nancy and George lurched up to the twelfth floor. With a loud clang, the door opened onto an enormous loft.

"There you are," Kate said, sweeping across

the stone floor. She was still in leggings but had changed to a bright paisley shirt. "I'm so glad you made it."

Nancy introduced George, and then Kate took them over to the piano in the sitting area, where a small group of people were gathered. She introduced Nancy and George, then said, "Okay, gals, you're on your own. Follow your noses to the buffet, make yourselves comfortable, and have fun."

"You're the one who saved Jason," a pretty young brunette said. "I'm Darcy Lane." Nancy recognized her from magazine ads.

"That was some accident," another model said.

"How do we know it was an accident?" Darcy said with a big grin. "Maybe Miranda tipped the trophy over on purpose."

"I wouldn't put it past her," the second girl muttered.

"Now, girls," a tall man said, joining the crowd. Nancy judged him to be about thirty-five years old, although his wavy hair was prematurely silver. The man turned to Nancy and George. "Hi. I'm Jack Herman."

"I remember you from the shoot," Nancy said. "You're the photographer."

"Guilty," he answered. "You two hungry? Let's hit the buffet." Nancy and George followed him to the tables of food laid out in the dining area. They helped themselves to the array of meats, cheeses, and salads that filled one long table.

"Is this your first Indy 500?" Jack asked.

"Yes, and it's so exciting," Nancy answered.

"How about you?" George asked.

"I've been twice," Jack said. "Once as a spectator and once as a photographer for *SportsTime* magazine." He led them to a small table with three chairs.

Nancy was about to speak when there was a stir at the edge of the room. Nancy glanced over and saw Miranda Marott, dressed in flashy fuchsia vinyl. She strode over to Darcy and immediately began putting down a top designer's new teen line.

"It's all junk," Miranda said with a sneer. She sat down gracefully, crossing her long, curvy legs and smoothing the micro-skirt of her dress. "I wouldn't be caught dead wearing *any* of it."

As Nancy headed back to the buffet table for an extra napkin, Miranda caught her eye. "Speaking of being caught dead, look who's here," the model said. "Jason's heroine. Well, thanks for nothing."

"Shut up, Miranda," Darcy said. "You don't mean that."

"Don't tell me what I mean!" Miranda snapped, her green eyes flashing as she flounced away.

"Miranda hates Jason," Darcy told Nancy.

"Why?" Nancy asked, seating herself on the ottoman next to the blond model.

"They got off on the wrong foot. Miranda is used to being the queen wherever she goes, and Jason doesn't bow and scrape."

"Where is he, anyway?" Kate asked, joining the group. "He should be here by now." She sat down in a huge velvet chair next to Nancy. "Jason hasn't been himself lately," she said with a sigh.

"What do you mean?" Nancy asked.

"Oh, I don't know—nervous, edgy," Kate said. "He always seems to be looking over his shoulder," Kate said, "as if he's expecting some kind of trouble."

"And he almost got it," Miranda said, rejoining them.

Nancy wondered whether Jason had had a premonition about the accident—or maybe it wasn't an accident. She remembered the rippling curtain just before the trophy fell. Maybe Jason *was* expecting trouble.

Where could he be? she wondered. Excusing herself, Nancy stood up and strolled around the huge loft, asking if anyone knew where Jason was. No one did.

As Nancy circled the far end of the loft, she reached the sleeping area, which was partitioned off by hanging rugs and screens. Glancing through a space between screens, Nancy saw two models primping at a large dressing table.

"Boy, Miranda is especially obnoxious tonight," one of them said.

"She's always that way," the second model said.

"Yes, but it's worse lately. She's driving me nuts. I think Kate's sorry she ever hired her."

"Well, you know what I heard? I was in New York last week, and the talk there is that Miranda's reign is nearly over."

"You're kidding! Who says?"

"Everybody. What's more, it doesn't look as if she's going to be able to move up to being an adult star, either. She's too much trouble."

"That'll be a blow. I've heard she's got mountains of debts."

Nancy walked back to the table where George and Jack sat. "Any chance I could see the contact sheet from the shoot this morning?" she asked Jack casually.

"Well, I don't know," he said curiously. "Why?"

"I'm an amateur photographer," Nancy explained, smiling. "I'd like to see what results you got."

"A photographer, hmm?" he said. "Well, if

you're really a colleague, I suppose . . ." His eyes narrowed as he studied her. "Sure, why not," he said finally, smiling at Nancy and George. He put down his plate and glanced around the room. "How about right now? My studio is just a block away. We can go and be back before anyone misses us."

Nancy, George, and Jack slipped out of Kate's loft and down Conner Street to a ground-floor loft. "It's a six-room apartment," Jack explained. "Four workrooms and a two-room living area in the back."

The studio space was large and messy. Stacks of contact sheets slopped over two desks, punctuated by a box of slides, a viewer, or a lens. Tripods and light poles leaned in corners, and a light box and projector covered a drafting board.

"I make no apologies for the mess," Jack said. Skillfully, he guided them along a path between magazines, cans of developing fluid, and packages of paper that littered the floor. Nancy noticed a door in the corner with a large Keep Out sign tacked to it.

"Here's the contact sheet from the shoot," Jack said, handing the large paper to Nancy. Horizontal rows of small photos stretched across the sheet. Jack gave her a photographer's magnifier, called a loupe.

She placed the magnifier over the contact sheet, carefully studying the tiny photos.

"What's this?" she asked abruptly. "What's this dark place?" She pointed to one of the proofs.

One strip of shots had been taken just before the trophy fell. Four were nearly alike, but the fifth had a dark, shadowy image along the side of the pedestal. It could have been a person, but it was hard to tell.

Jack peered through the small lens. "Let's blow it up," he said.

While Jack went into the developing room behind the Keep Out sign, Nancy called the number Kate had given her for Jason's flat. After four rings, she could hear Jason's nasal voice saying, "This is a machine. You know what to do—do it."

She left a message asking Jason to call her room when he returned.

When Jack finally stuck his head out of the darkroom, he said, "Come see what you think." Eagerly, Nancy and George went into the darkened developing room.

The room glowed with a spooky red light. Three wet blowups swung eerily from a drying line—the shot that Nancy had requested plus the two before. Peering carefully at the first picture, Nancy saw a slight shadow by the pedestal, but it was difficult to make out exactly what it was.

Nancy looked at the next photograph. The shadow was darker and more defined—it looked as if a person was lurking behind and a little to the side of the pedestal.

The third blowup solved the puzzle. The edge of someone's body did show. Only half of the face was revealed.

"Do you know who this is?" Nancy asked Jack. "Maybe someone from the photo or fashion crew?"

"No," Jack murmured. "Of course, I don't know everyone who works for Kate. People come and go pretty regularly."

"May I borrow this?" Nancy asked. "I want Kate to take a look at it."

"Sure. Let me know if you need anything else," Jack said as he locked the small building. The three walked back to Kate's loft.

"There you are," Miranda said as Nancy, George, and Jack stepped back into Kate's living room. "We were wondering where you guys had gone."

"Don't tell me you missed me," Jack said, casually slipping an arm around Miranda's tiny waist. "I'd find that hard to believe."

"I'll bet he took you girls on a tour of the famous Jack Herman studio," Miranda said to

Nancy and George. "What a mess that place is. It's a wonder he gets any work done at all."

"I haven't heard any complaints, my dear," Jack said. "In fact, *you* always look especially great in my shots."

Miranda struck an exaggerated pose. "That may be, but—"

"What? No!" Kate's shriek pierced the airy room.

Nancy, with George and Jack close behind her, followed the sound to the kitchen, where Kate stood holding the phone. Her face was ashen, her dark brown eyes wide with shock. "Who is this?" she demanded into the phone. "How do you know?" Then she dropped the receiver to the counter.

Kate stood still, her face pale, hands shaking. "Jason . . . Jason," she murmured.

"Jason called?" Jack asked. "It's about time."

"No, it—it wasn't Jason," Kate stammered. "I don't know who it was. The voice was muffled. A man's . . . he hung up."

"What did he say?" Nancy asked gently.

Kate turned to Nancy, her eyes brimming with tears. "He said Jason's been murdered!"

Chapter

Five

"Murdered!" Nancy repeated softly. She was shocked by Kate's revelation.

"Who's been murdered?" Darcy asked. "You're kidding, right?"

"Who was it?" Jack asked. "What's happened?"

"I—I—don't know," Kate stammered. Without another word, she hurried to the back of the loft, to the shelter of her bedroom behind the Chinese screens.

Nancy slipped away from the group and followed Kate. When she reached the screens, she called out softly, "Kate? Is there anything I can do?"

Kate stepped out from behind a vividly

painted tiger screen. Her arms were folded tightly across her chest, and her eyes were wide with fear. "I don't know who was on the phone," she told Nancy, her voice shaky. "The voice was muffled. He hung up right away."

As George joined Nancy, Kate crumpled into a chair, her shoulders trembling.

"He didn't tell you how he knew?" George asked the young designer.

Kate shook her head, then sighed. "What kind of animal would give me such horrible news and then hang up?" she asked. "And why?"

"Someone cruel," George suggested.

"Not necessarily," Nancy said, handing Kate a tissue. "It could have been someone phoning in a tip. He knows what happened and wants to help but doesn't want to be identified."

"Or he might be afraid of the murderer," George added.

"Murderer!" Kate gasped. "I just can't believe it."

Nancy flashed a warning glance at George. "Look," Nancy said, turning to Kate. "We don't know if it's true or not. It could be a horrible prank. If you'd like, I can look into it."

"Nancy's a detective," George told Kate. "She's solved many cases."

"Would you help me, Nancy?" Kate pleaded.

"I'd like to keep this out of the papers if it's a crank call. It has to be—it just *has* to be. Of course, if it's true . . ." A glistening tear slid down her cheek.

"I'll see what I can find out," Nancy said. "Meanwhile, you'd better report the call to the police."

While Kate made the call from the kitchen phone, Nancy passed around the photo blowup showing the person partially hidden by the trophy pedestal. No one could make an identification.

After a few minutes, Kate approached Nancy. "I just spoke to Officer Washington," Kate explained. "He told me there wasn't much the police could do at this point, but if I get any more calls, I should let him or his partner know."

"Where does Jason live?" Nancy asked. "I'd like to check out his place." Kate drew a small map on the back of a napkin. "Don't worry," Nancy told the frightened designer. "Maybe it was just a crank call."

Nancy watched as Kate was consoled by a group of models. Then she turned to George, saying, "Come on, let's get out of here."

"Do you think the phone call was a prank?" George asked once they were back in Nancy's car.

"I don't know," Nancy answered. "If it was, then who called—and why?" She thought for a moment, then added, "Let's run by Jason's. Maybe he's home safe and sound, and the whole mystery will be solved."

Jason's apartment was in a restored brownstone on a cobblestone street, lit by old-fashioned globe street lamps. As Nancy and George approached the front stairs of the brownstone, they heard only the trickle of water from a copper fountain in the courtyard outside the house. Other than that, there was total silence.

Inside the foyer, Nancy pressed the buzzer above Jason's mailbox a couple of times. There was no response. The door between the foyer and the inside hallway had two glass panels.

Nancy peered through the door. Only six steps led up to Jason's door on the second floor at the top of the stairs. A newspaper and a couple of packages lay on the straw mat outside his door.

"Sure looks like he's not home," George said.

Nancy and George walked back out of the building and around to the alley that ran along one side of the building. They'd gone only a few steps when Nancy noticed that one of Jason's windows was open just a crack.

She glanced around. "I'm going in," she said.

"You keep watch, George. You can see the front walk from here—give a whistle if you see anyone coming."

"No way," George said. "I'm going in with you."

Nancy could tell by the expression on her friend's face that she was not going to change her mind. "All right, but this is going to be a quick look."

Carefully, noiselessly, Nancy placed a plastic trash can under the window. She sat on the lid, giving it a trial run for strength, then hoisted herself up until she was standing and could reach the open window.

Nancy pushed the window up slowly. After pausing to make sure she heard no sounds inside the apartment, she boosted herself over the sill and dropped down inside the bathroom.

Nancy went back to the window and motioned to George to come up.

Her heart racing, Nancy pulled the bathroom door open all the way and stepped into a short hall. George followed closely behind.

The silence was eerie. Nancy's skin felt clammy as she remembered the phone message to Kate. "Be careful," she whispered to George. "If Jason has been murdered, there's no telling what we might find here."

"Are you saying that if we open a closet,

Jason's corpse might fall out?" George asked. Her dark eyes were wide as she looked behind her.

"Just be careful."

An involuntary shudder rippled across Nancy's shoulders as she led George through the kitchen and dining room and into the living room.

The heavy drapes were closed so that only slivers of light around the edges pierced the room. Everything looked fine. Nothing seemed disturbed or out of place.

Backtracking down the hall, Nancy and George reached what looked like a study or home office. Nancy raced straight for the desk and was relieved to see by the various envelopes and papers stacked neatly around that the apartment did belong to Jason Randell.

"It wouldn't be cool for us to break and enter the wrong place," she murmured with a half smile.

"What are we looking for?" George asked in a loud whisper.

"Something that will tell us why Jason felt edgy, something that showed he was in danger—a threatening message, a diary entry."

Nancy shuffled quickly through Jason's papers, searching for a clue to where he might be or what might have happened to him. On his answering machine were only Nancy's message and several frantic calls from Kate.

Nancy thumbed through files and a looseleaf notebook containing requisition orders for Kate's firm. Every order had an original sheet and a copy. On a hunch, she took out the copy for each order for April and May, folded them, and stuffed them in her pocket.

"Here's something," Nancy said. She picked up a pocket-size electronic reminder. "This is one of those pocket computers—not much memory, but good for keeping track of appointments, telephone numbers, and stuff like that."

She turned it on and flipped through Jason's appointments for May.

"Find anything?" George asked.

"Mostly notes about the fashion shoot and the Be a Sport! line. Mmm, I wonder what this means—'Introduce BP.' Here's another— 'Time for BP.'"

"What's a BP?"

"Or who? It may be someone's initials." Nancy scanned through the rest of Jason's pocket reminder. "He has some things scheduled for next week," she added, making a few notes in her notebook. "I hope he's still able to do them."

She turned on Jason's computer and began

scanning his files. "Why don't you check out the bedroom while I do this?" Nancy said.

Nancy grabbed a blank disk from a box in the desk drawer and copied onto it the files that related to Kate's business—schedules, databases of models and suppliers, notes about the Be a Sport! launch.

There was one short file labeled simply "BP." She copied that too, then shut down the computer and headed for the bedroom.

In contrast to the tidy office, the bedroom was messy. "I haven't found anything that might help, but I haven't checked the closet yet," George said. "Not very neat, is he?"

"Maybe he left in a hurry," Nancy said. "Or was dragged out . . ."

She looked quickly through the bedroom but found no clues. When she opened the closet, Nancy saw a note stuck to the mirror inside the door: "Push K about BP."

"Listen," George said suddenly. "Do you hear that?" Nancy felt her nerves hop to attention as she stopped to listen. The sound of muffled voices penetrated the dusty dimness of the apartment.

"Someone's in the hall outside the flat. Quick—back to the bathroom," Nancy whispered urgently. She gave George a little push and followed her into the hallway leading to the bathroom. The voices were growing louder—they were right outside the apartment, but she still couldn't tell what they were saying.

George disappeared into the bathroom. As Nancy sprinted down the hall, she heard the unmistakable sound of a key turning in the front door lock.

Chapter
Six

As THE KEY TURNED in the front door of Jason's apartment, Nancy popped into the bathroom, pulling the door almost closed. George headed for the window, while Nancy lingered at the door.

"Mr. Randell? Mr. Randell, are you in here?" a woman's voice called from the living room. "It's Mrs. Manion, your landlady, and two police officers." There was quiet for a few moments, then Nancy heard the voice again. "I tell you I haven't seen him for a couple of days."

Nancy thought she recognized the second voice as that of Officer Washington, the police officer who had questioned her after the trophy accident.

"Okay," Mrs. Manion said. "I'll be downstairs if you need me."

The door closed, then Nancy heard Detective Cook's distinctive drawl. "Seems like the super's right, Brant. Doesn't look like anyone's here."

"Let's check it out anyway," Officer Washington said. "You look around in here; I'll take the bedroom."

Her pulse pounding in her temples, Nancy crept to the bathroom window. Behind her, she could hear Officer Washington's footsteps in the hall. She urged George through the window first and then eased herself out, dropping silently onto the rigid plastic trash can.

Nancy didn't stop to close the window. She and George tore down the alley to the street.

Quickly, they scrambled into the Mustang. Only after she had driven a block did Nancy take a real breath. "That was too close," she said with a shudder. "The police were the same two that talked to me out at the track after the trophy fell."

"Wouldn't be too cool to have them catch you snooping around two different places in one day," George said with a teasing glint in her eye.

"Hey, give me a break. I'm on a case," Nancy said as she pulled the car into a parking place at the Barbary Inn. "Kate asked for my help, remember?"

In the parlor, the innkeeper, Alice Froman, put down her embroidery and greeted Nancy with a wad of phone messages.

Nancy thanked her and sifted through the messages. Kate had phoned several times and urgently wanted Nancy to return her calls. Then Jack Herman had called to say he had finished blowups for her of the trophy shoot if she needed them. Frank had phoned to say they had a guaranteed parking spot near Killer Hill on the minimarathon route. One of Robbie's crew members lived there and was letting them park in his driveway. And finally, Officer Washington had called to check a few points in Nancy's account of the near disaster at the fashion shoot.

"Too bad," George said with a mock frown when she heard about the last message. "If you'd known he was trying to get hold of you, you could have talked to him at Jason's."

"Oh, right," Nancy said with a grin as she dialed the phone.

She hoped it wasn't too late to return calls. She tried Kate first because she thought she'd still be up after her party. It was obvious from her voice that the vivacious young designer was in a better mood. She told Nancy that she had convinced herself Jason was all right.

"He's kind of nuts sometimes," she said. "Really—he's probably behind this whole crank call thing. Just to get back at me for pushing him too hard at work. This way, he can get a little time to himself for a while. He'll probably turn up in a few days, yelling 'Gotcha!' at me."

"Are you sure?" Nancy asked doubtfully. "Telling someone you've been murdered seems kind of extreme for a practical joke."

"Not for Jason, believe me," Kate said with a laugh. "As I said, he can be pretty wacky. I'm sure there's no need for worry. Did you go to his place?"

"Yes," Nancy said, "but we didn't see him." She decided not to tell Kate about breaking into Jason's apartment.

"Well, I'm sorry our little evening was ruined. Let me make it up to you. My friend and financial backer, Leon Goldman, is giving a big party tomorrow evening at his estate, and he's asked me to be his hostess. I hope you and George will be able to come—feel free to bring dates."

"Sounds wonderful," Nancy said. "Let me check with George." Holding her hand over the receiver, Nancy repeated Kate's invitation. George nodded enthusiastically. "We'll be there," Nancy said to Kate on the phone.

"Good! There should be lots of exciting people there—drivers, celebrities. Who knows, Jason might even show up." Kate gave Nancy instructions on how to get to Leon Goldman's house.

"Great," Nancy said. "We'll see you there tomorrow."

After Kate hung up, Nancy told George what Kate had said.

"She thinks Jason faked this whole episode to get back at his devoted friend and boss?" George asked. "Wow. I'm glad he's not *my* pal."

"You and me both," Nancy said. She picked up the phone and decided to try Officer Washington. Even though his shift should have been over, he had been at Jason's apartment. When Washington answered, he explained that he had pulled an extra detail. He said he wanted to verify that she had seen the curtain move prior to the trophy accident.

Nancy repeated what she had told him earlier, then asked, "Have you turned up any information on the supposed murder of Jason Randell? I was with Kate Cordova when she got the call."

"Are you always where the action is, Ms. Drew? Actually, Ms. Cordova called back a few minutes ago and said she was sure it was a hoax—perhaps perpetrated by Mr. Randell himself. Well, goodbye," he said, closing off any further questions. "Thank you for returning my call."

"This whole thing is very odd," Nancy said quietly as she hung up.

The next morning was cool and dry—perfect marathon weather. Joe awoke early, excited and eager for the challenge of racing thirteen miles.

He showered quickly. After drying off, he smeared a thin layer of petroleum jelly on his feet before pulling on his socks. It would keep his feet from blistering during the race.

By the time Frank was out of the shower, Joe already had on his neon orange racing shorts and white singlet. He pinned his racing number onto the singlet and pulled on a white visor, then did a few warm-up stretches while Frank dressed.

After a twenty-minute drive, they arrived at the Barbary Inn and picked up Nancy and George.

Once the girls were buckled in, Frank drove downtown toward Monument Circle, in the heart of Indianapolis. Racers packed the circle, a brick rotary with four streets leading out from it—north, south, east, and west—like the spokes of a wheel. Frank pulled the van to a stop.

"Good luck," Nancy said as Joe hopped out. "Have a great run."

"All the pros have the prime positions up front," Joe said, stretching on the sidewalk nearby. "But I'm not too far back. I should have a shot at a personal best."

Members of the press milled around, taping shots and jotting notes. Friends and family members cheered and waved as the racers began taking their places in the huge crowd.

Joe jogged over to the other runners and did some more leg stretches.

The start of the race seemed slow to Joe as thousands of runners began to move up Meridian Street. But soon the international marathon stars who led the pack sprinted ahead, and the slower runners fell back or moved to the sides. Then the more serious ones—like Joe—made their moves.

He got into his rhythm and was feeling great. After ten blocks, the route turned west, heading through neighborhoods of close-set bungalows. What looked like three generations of families thronged each of the porches and stoops, cheering on the runners.

At the first water station, Joe downed water and sponged the back of his neck without missing a stride. He threw the empty cup and sponge out to the curb and smiled at the pretty teenage girl who retrieved them.

After a few miles, a man in his twenties tried to move up on Joe's left, but Joe turned up the burners a little and left him behind easily.

Finally, Joe could see Killer Hill ahead. He

knew that once the hill was conquered, it would be only minutes before he reached the Speedway. The minimarathon was the only time pedestrians were allowed on the famous track.

"Hey, Joe!" He heard Nancy's voice calling out to him. She, Frank, and George cheered from the sidewalk and waved as he passed them.

As he started up the hill, he felt his pulse pound in his throat, partially masking the sounds around him—crowd cheers, the purring motors of camera dollies, the *slap-slap* of his shoes on the asphalt.

Then a new sound whistled by. With mounting horror, Joe identified the sound. His pulse sped up. It was the *zing* of a bullet whizzing by his ear.

Chapter

Seven

THE BULLET WHISTLED past Joe's head, then pierced the windshield of a car parked in a driveway off Killer Hill.

Joe and the other front-runners dove for safety behind trees and bushes. For a few seconds, most of the spectators and race volunteers didn't move—they were in shock. Then a man yelled, "Someone's got a gun! Get down!"

Some people dropped instantly, flattening themselves on the sidewalks and grassy lawns lining the race route. Others darted in all directions, slamming into one another or stumbling and falling.

Joe scrambled to a more sheltered spot behind a bushy shrub.

"Joe! Joe!" Frank called as he ran toward the shrub. "Are you okay?"

"Yeah, I'm fine. Just a little shook up. Did you see where the bullet came from?"

"Not really," Frank said, crouching. "Maybe from that roof." He pointed across the street.

Police swarmed all over Killer Hill. Several volunteers stopped other marathoners before they started their ascent. A voice boomed a monotone message through a bullhorn: "The race is officially declared over. Please leave the area. Everyone leave the area now."

"Where are the girls?" Joe asked his brother, looking around.

"They're over by the water station." Joe glanced over and saw George and Nancy kneeling behind a bench with a few other spectators.

Frank looked back at the flat roof where he thought the sniper might have been located. Two police officers ran across the roof, checking behind chimneys and the air-conditioner unit. One gave out a yell and held up a rifle.

A few minutes passed with no more shots fired. "I think it's over," Joe said.

"Looks like they got the gun, anyway," Frank said, standing up slowly.

Police started herding people out of the area. Frank and Joe joined Nancy and George at the water station.

"Did you see anything?" Nancy asked.

"Not really," Frank said. "How about you?"

"Nothing," Nancy said. "We talked to a few spectators, but no one saw anything."

"Please leave the area, folks." An officer gestured to the four friends to move away.

"We're heading over to the track," Frank said to Nancy and George. "You two want to come? Maybe we can sneak you into the garage area for a tour."

"Sure, we'd love to," Nancy said, and George nodded enthusiastically.

But first they all stopped at the Hardys' motel so Joe could shower and change. Frank told Nancy and George about the fight that Robbie had had with Jean-Claude Rochefort, and then talk turned to the sniper.

"Why do you suppose he—or she—did it?" George asked. "Just a nut?"

"Maybe," Frank said. "There are a lot of crazies out there."

"It was scary how close that bullet came to Joe," Nancy pointed out. "Do you think Joe could actually have been the target?"

"I've been wondering that myself." Joe emerged from the bedroom in jeans and a blue-striped rugby shirt. "First the race car, now this," he continued, pulling on his sneakers.

"But the track thing was an accident, wasn't it?" George asked.

"Maybe," Frank said, heading toward the

closet. "And maybe not." He took a package out of the closet, unwrapped it, and held out the broken suspension rod. "What do you think, Nancy? Broken or cut?"

"I can't tell exactly," Nancy said, running her finger across the end, "but there are definitely two textures on that end. So it either broke two different ways—"

"Pretty unlikely," Joe muttered.

"—or it was cut halfway and broke the rest," Nancy concluded.

"But no one knew you were going to be driving the race car, right?" George asked.

"Exactly," Joe said. "Everyone thought it would be Robbie, so it fits the team sabotage theory."

"If someone sabotaged the car, it had to be someone who could get into the garage, right?" Nancy asked.

"Exactly," Joe said.

"So you may be talking about a team member," George said. "Whoa, that's bad."

"Knocking off Joe during the marathon doesn't fit, though," Nancy said.

"Unless someone's onto us," Joe said, "and knows that we're working undercover. Everyone on the team knew I was going to be running the minimarathon today."

"Do you really suspect someone on your own team?" Nancy asked.

"Maybe someone who used to be," Frank added as they walked out to the van. Frank told Nancy and George about Giovanni Randisi.

"How about giving us a hand with our investigation?" Joe said with a grin. "It'll keep you out of trouble."

"Actually, we have a mystery of our own shaping up," Nancy said.

As they headed for the track, Nancy told the Hardys about Kate's phone call and checking out Jason's apartment.

"By the way, we're invited to a big party tonight," Nancy said as they waited to turn into the tunnel that ran under the track. "Not too formal. It's at Leon Goldman's estate. He's Kate's financial backer and—"

"Leon Goldman!" Joe interrupted. *"The* Leon Goldman? The U.S. Olympic Committee Leon Goldman?"

"And also owner of Jean-Claude Rochefort's racing team," Frank added.

"No kidding," Nancy said. "That means Randisi will be there. How about coming as our escorts?"

"Absolutely," Joe said. "Wouldn't miss it."

"But tomorrow is qualification day, and we report to Robbie's garage at six-thirty in the morning," Frank warned.

"So we'll make an early evening of it," Joe said. "In bed by ten-thirty, okay?"

"Right," Frank said. "I knew there was some reason why we packed those sports jackets."

"There probably won't be too much action on the track today," Frank commented. "It was officially closed to cars so that the marathoners could take their laps. Most of the mechanics planned to fine-tune their cars today, and the drivers have several charity events to attend."

Above them they heard the deafening, exhilarating noise of an Indy race car zooming over their heads.

"Someone's out there," Joe said. "They must have opened it back up for practice."

When they arrived at Gasoline Alley, Joe and Frank showed the yellow-shirted guard their badges.

"What about them?" the guard asked, pointing to Nancy and George.

"They're with us," Frank said.

"They got to have passes," the guard said.

"Come on," Joe said. "It's a slow day because of the marathon. You can let them through."

"No way," the man said. "Since that sniper attack, security is tighter than ever."

As Joe continued to plead their case, Frank saw Robbie walking to his garage and honked to get his attention. Personal guests of the drivers were always admitted, and Robbie waved them through immediately.

Robbie followed them to their parking place, then opened the back door of the van and took George's hand to help her out. "Okay, I got them in," he said to the Hardys. "Now return the favor and introduce me to these lovely young ladies."

Robbie shook Nancy's hand and flashed her his magnetic smile. A green T-shirt showed off his muscular upper body. When he took George's hand, he didn't let go.

"You've been holding out on me, crew," Robbie said, "but we'll just have to make up for all that lost time." He gazed directly into George's eyes. "We'll start with dinner tonight."

"Sorry, old man," Joe said, slipping an arm around George's waist. "She's my date tonight. We're all attending the big blast at Leon Goldman's."

"You travel in pretty fancy circles," Robbie said, letting go of George. "Don't forget you report to my garage at six-thirty A.M. By the way, I got an invitation to Goldman's myself—all the drivers did."

He turned back to George and gave her a warm smile. "I didn't intend to go, but if you're going, that's good enough for me. In fact, I hope you'll all accompany me there in my limo."

"Sounds great," George said in a low voice.

"Well, if my date is going in the limo, I guess I'd better, too," Joe said with a crooked smile.

Robbie's stretch limo arrived at the Barbary Inn at ten after seven. Earlier, Kate had sent over a few of her designs for Nancy and George to choose from for the party. Nancy picked a two-piece blue outfit with a halter top and short skirt. George chose a straight black shift with shoulder straps.

Nancy and George headed down the walkway of the inn toward the limo. Robbie, dressed in black jeans and a white dinner jacket, opened the door for the girls. Once inside, he made no secret of his interest in George and made sure she sat next to him.

After picking up the Hardys, they headed north to the Goldman estate, a two-hundred-fifty-acre horse farm of rolling meadows marked off with white fences, formal gardens, perfect lawns, and a manor house built in the style of a French chateau.

The limo was directed to a parking area near the tennis courts. There were three huge party houses on the back lawn. One had a dance floor and a band, one had tables for dining, and one was for meeting and mingling.

Robbie led the Hardys, Nancy, and George to the bar in the last party house. He ordered sodas for everyone, while Nancy and the others loaded their plates with shrimp, cheese spreads and crackers, and meatballs.

"Nancy! George! I'm so glad you could make it." Kate Cordova joined them with a swirl of her bright red chiffon skirt. With her was a tall, distinguished-looking man who Nancy guessed was in his forties. He had a stocky build, dark hair flecked with silver, and piercing green eyes. "I'd like you to meet Leon Goldman."

After introductions were made, Mr. Goldman turned to Joe, his eyes narrowing to slits under dark bushy brows. "You're the mechanic who drove one of the Brandon cars, aren't you?"

"I took full responsibility, Leon," Robbie said. "You know that—and you know I paid for it."

"Perhaps not enough," Mr. Goldman said, turning his dark gaze on Robbie.

"Come on," Kate said, taking Mr. Goldman's hand and giving him a loving look. "These are your guests. Please, let's make them welcome."

Mr. Goldman's expression softened. He turned to Nancy and the others and smiled warmly. "Forgive me," he said. "I tend to take the office with me wherever I go. Enjoy the party." With a squeeze of Kate's hand, he walked off.

"Sorry," Kate said sheepishly. "He's really a

wonderful man, but he gets kind of crazy every year during the month of May and the Indy 500."

"I know the feeling," Robbie said, smiling.

Kate pulled Nancy away for a moment, telling her that she had not heard from Jason. She added that because his body hadn't turned up, she was sure it was one of his macabre jokes.

She bounced off, saying, "I'd better join Leon and greet our guests. Have fun. We'll talk later."

Nancy filled the others in on what Kate had said, and then they milled around for a while. It was an impressive guest list—sports heroes, entertainment superstars, media giants, and corporate presidents moved in and out of the party houses and across the lush grounds.

Finally, the guests took seats at the dining tables in the center party house. As a string quartet began playing, dozens of waiters served the first course of lobster mousse and crab legs.

Nancy, George, the Hardys, and Robbie were seated at a table just in front of the head table, where Mr. Goldman, Kate, Jean-Claude Rochefort, a rock superstar, a national network anchorman, and a few other recognizable celebrities sat.

Mr. Goldman stood to propose a toast. "Thank you all for coming," he said. "I would like to begin by saying that none of this would have been possible without the superb planning of my dear, elegant Kate." He turned to her, raising his champagne glass. "So here's to—"

"Excuse us. Please step aside." The toast was interrupted by two men in dark suits who were pushing their way through waiters and guests until they reached the head table. One mumbled into a handheld remote unit. They stopped beside Kate's chair.

"Are you Kate Sylvana Cordova?" one asked.

"Yes, yes I am," Kate answered. She looked surprised and confused.

"What is going on here?" Mr. Goldman demanded. "Security," he called. "We need some security here."

"Calm down, Mr. Goldman," the intruder said. "This doesn't concern you. If you'll stand, please, Miss Cordova, and come with us. We can explain this outside and in private."

"See here, let her go!" Mr. Goldman yelled. "You have no right—"

"I am Treasury Agent Ron Albright, and I have every right," the man said, bristling. He flashed a badge, then pulled Kate up from her chair. "Miss Cordova, you are being taken into federal custody for smuggling jewels into the United States."

Chapter

Eight

"SMUGGLING JEWELS!" Leon Goldman boomed, his voice rattling around the party house. "That's absurd. Release her at once."

"I'm afraid we can't do that," Agent Albright said. He slipped handcuffs on Kate's wrists and guided her ahead of him toward the door.

Kate glanced back, first at Leon Goldman, then at Nancy. She looked scared. A buzz hummed around the room as guests sitting at tables farther back were told what was happening. Mr. Goldman, murmuring into his cellular phone, stormed after the government agent.

Nancy followed them outside. "Kate!" she called. "Is there anything I can do?"

"Thank you, but we don't need your help,

Ms. Drew," Mr. Goldman said firmly. "This is merely a misunderstanding."

The men ushered Kate into an Indianapolis police car as Leon Goldman stomped off to his house.

Nancy was unable to work her way through the crowd to return to her table. Within minutes George, Robbie, and the Hardys joined Nancy outside.

"Did you get to talk to her?" George asked.

"No—Mr. Goldman brushed me off," Nancy said. "I wonder where they're taking her. They drove off in a city police car. They're probably going to the jail."

Some guests were still talking, while others headed for their cars. "Well, it's nine o'clock, and tomorrow is qualifications," Frank said. "Joe, let's hit the sack early. We want to do everything we can to put Robbie in the pole position tomorrow."

"In the front row?" Robbie said. "I'd have to be the top qualifier. It'd sure be great if we could swing it. Actually, I'll be happy if I get in the front three rows. That would make me one of the nine fastest qualifiers. Most of the last thirty races were won by someone in one of those positions."

He turned to George. "You'll be there tomorrow?"

"You couldn't keep me away," George answered. "We're supposed to join Kate in the Goldman suite, but I don't know now. . . ." She looked at Nancy.

"We'll be there," Nancy assured them. "George, let's leave now, too. It doesn't seem right to party without the hosts."

Back at the Barbary Inn, Nancy and George checked the requisition copies and computer records Nancy had copied in Jason's flat the night before.

First, they examined the copies of the order sheets for Kate's design studio. Fabric, thread, accessories, buttons—all were carefully recorded. All the sheets seemed complete with dates, addresses, broker names, and Kate's signature at the bottom.

"Looks like Kate uses nothing but the best," George said. "Silks from Asia, leather from Italy, wools and linens from Britain."

Nancy looked closely at one sheet labeled simply Accessories, then showed it to George. She pointed to the boxes marked Quantity, Amount per Unit, and Total Amount. "The numbers are impossible to read," she declared.

"The carbon ink must have smudged."

"Maybe." Nancy noted the supplier's name was Silvio of Florence, Italy.

"This must be why I brought my laptop," Nancy said, lifting the lid of the computer.

"You're on another working vacation," George said with a smile.

Nancy checked the computer disk with Jason's copied files. She pulled up the BP file, but it was scrambled and she didn't know the password.

Then she looked at the models' directory. Each model had a separate file. Miranda's was the largest.

"Darcy wasn't kidding when she said Jason and Miranda didn't get along," Nancy said. The file was filled with accounts of problems and confrontations between Jason and Miranda.

There were also frequent notes to and from Kate about firing Miranda or not hiring her. Jason had written memos over the past year urging Kate to pass over Miranda and use someone else as the star of Be a Sport! "B.P. might be the model Jason wanted Kate to hire to replace Miranda," Nancy said.

"Maybe Miranda arranged for something to happen to Jason," George offered. "She might have been worried that he was trying to get her fired."

"The models say she's in trouble financially," Nancy said. She closed her computer and tumbled into her high bed by the window.

"Well, it wouldn't surprise me if she had hired someone to take out Jason," George said, climbing into the other bed. Within minutes both girls were fast asleep.

Saturday morning was perfect, with bright sunshine and a clear sky. Kate called to tell Nancy that she had been released on bail and still expected Nancy and George in Mr. Goldman's track suite for qualifications.

After she hung up, Nancy called Officer Washington. "I just thought I'd see if any leads had turned up on Jason Randell," she said.

"No," Officer Washington said. "Until there's a body, we're treating it as a missing person. Thank you for calling, Miss Drew. Goodbye." He hung up abruptly.

The morning paper's lead story was all about Kate's arrest. Over Alice Froman's raspberry scones, Nancy shared the article with George. "It says here that the jewels were sewn into the linings of custom-made leather bags from Italy," Nancy said, scanning the article. "Remember the smudged order sheet for accessories from Silvio of Florence?"

George nodded thoughtfully as Nancy opened her computer again. Punching a few keys, Nancy tried to send an E-mail to Silvio, but she received a message telling her there was no such address. Then she checked Jason's supplier database file for Silvio and discovered that it listed the same address and telephone number.

"That's odd," Nancy said. "Let's check this address with Kate when we get to the track."

"They're saying it'll take a four-lap qualifying average of two hundred twenty-five miles per hour to make the field this year," Joe said, his excitement mounting as he parked next to the Brandon garage.

"And two thirty-six or better to get the pole," Frank said, shaking his head with wonder.

Qualifications were always nearly as exciting as the race itself. Usually, the qualifying rounds were held on the second and third weekends of May, but because it had rained the past weekend, they were all being held this weekend.

All thirty-three places—eleven rows of three cars each—would be filled in just one weekend. In track terminology, the fastest qualifier would "sit on the pole," which was the left, or inside, slot in the first row. On race day, everyone else would line up after the pole sitter, ranked according to their qualifying speed. All the drivers would start the race together, and the faster their qualifying time, the closer they would be to the front of the pack.

"I'll bet we're the first to show up," Joe said. He checked his watch—it was six-fifteen.

"Man, I'm pumped. We're actually going to help Robbie qualify!"

The garage door was unlocked, and Frank and Joe stepped inside. "Well, hello," an unfamiliar voice said. "You must be the two new fellas."

The man stepped out of the shadows. He was an older, heavier version of Robbie, and he spoke with a thicker Scottish brogue. But he had the same blue eyes and dark red hair, though his was close-cropped, not wavy. "I'm Sandy MacDonnell."

"Our missing chief mechanic," Frank said.

"Not missing," Sandy said. "Just late."

"Welcome." Frank stepped forward to shake hands. "I'm Frank Hardy. This is my brother, Joe."

Joe shook Sandy's hand, saying, "It must have been some emergency to keep you away from all this."

"I had some business to attend to," Sandy said, frowning slightly.

"It must have been important," Joe said, "for you to miss the week before quals. How was Chicago?"

"Chicago?" Sandy said. "What do you mean?"

"Uh, nothing," Joe muttered as the rest of the crew began to file in. All were happy to see their chief, and there was a lot of back slapping and shoulder punching as they welcomed him.

"Sandy! You finally made it." Robbie grabbed his brother in a bear hug. "Why didn't you call? Why didn't you come to the motel?"

"I got in about two this morning and came straight here. I didn't want to wake you. You needed your sleep. I spent some time going over the car. Looks like the crew did a good job while I was gone."

"The best—but then you trained most of them."

"And don't you forget it," Sandy said, flashing the winning MacDonnell grin.

While Robbie changed into his racing uniform, Sandy met with the crew. He explained a couple of changes he had made in the engine settings, then walked them through starting the car, tire changes, and fueling.

"They drew numbers to decide the qualifying order," Sandy said. "Robbie will be eighth. As soon as the track opens, I want him out on it practicing. They close practice at noon, and qualifying begins at twelve fifty-five. Any questions? Okay. We're the best crew in the pits— let's show 'em what we can do!"

Sandy huddled with Robbie while the crew pushed the car out of the garage. When they got to the pit, the Hardys checked the tires. "Look at the crowd," Joe said. The stands were almost filled.

The track opened for practice, and Robbie headed right out. But he came back in after a few laps, complaining about a shimmy in the rear of the car. Sandy ordered a few adjustments, and Robbie charged back out for an improved run.

At noon all the cars were waved off the track and qualifications began. As the first car zoomed down Pit Row, Joe felt a rush as he remembered his wild ride.

"I could get used to this," Nancy said. She and George were standing on the balcony of Leon Goldman's plush third-floor suite. The elegant two- and three-room track suites were located in a separate building rising behind the stands and overlooking the front straightaway. Kate joined them, bringing sandwiches and sodas.

"How are you doing?" Nancy asked as she helped Kate arrange the food on a glass table. Everyone was dressed in black and white, the traditional colors of the Indy 500. Kate wore her usual leggings, with a white chiffon blouse. Nancy and George wore white jeans. Nancy had topped hers with a black- and white-striped blouse, George with a black shirt.

"I'm better," Kate answered. "Thank goodness Leon and his attorney helped me make bail so that I didn't have to spend the night down there." She gave an involuntary shudder. "The worst thing was the humiliation. I can't believe I was arrested—in front of all those people."

"The paper says the jewels were smuggled in leather bags," Nancy said.

"Yes, but I didn't order them. The police showed me a requisition with my signature, but I don't remember it at all."

Nancy thought of the copy she had taken from Jason's flat. "Who makes your bags for you?" Nancy asked.

"I usually go to Silvio of Florence."

"I've heard that name," Nancy said casually. "Is there really a person named Silvio?"

"There was, but I've never met him. Jason usually dealt with the manufacturers. I met Silvio's broker—the man who represents him—at a party once, but I don't remember his name. He was a gorgeous Frenchman—he wore a gold ring with the head of Cleopatra on his little finger."

"Were the bags with the jewels also made by Silvio?" George asked.

"I don't know," Kate said, sounding tired and anxious. "I still haven't seen those bags. I guess the police have them."

"I'm sorry," Nancy said. "I didn't mean to upset you. One last question—do you know anyone with the initials B.P.?"

Kate thought for a minute. "No, I don't think so."

As Nancy, George, and Kate munched on their sandwiches and watched the track action, they could hear Miranda's high-pitched voice coming from inside the suite.

"Jason was right," Kate muttered. "I should have dumped her. Some people will put up with anything from a superstar, but not me. I'll be glad when her Be a Sport! contract is finished."

"Miranda and Jason don't get along very well, do they?" Nancy asked.

"They hate each other. She really gets on his nerves, and she's the kind of person who loves to do that. She may be young, but don't ever turn your back on her. Once she knows your weak spot, you're done." Kate shook her head, then turned toward the suite. "Please find Jason, Nancy," Kate said with a sigh.

"Poor Kate," Nancy said. "This is supposed to be an exciting time—launching her new fashions. But suddenly her assistant disappears and may even be murdered, and she's arrested for jewel smuggling. It looks as if someone is trying to ruin her. We've got to find out who."

"Don't worry, Nan, we will," George said

soothingly. She leaned over the balcony. "Look! There's Robbie. He'll be qualifying pretty soon. I sure wish I were down there in the action."

"What action?" Nancy said with a teasing look in her blue eyes. "Does it have anything to do with a certain hot Scottish driver?" Nancy laughed as George blushed. Nancy peered into her tote. "Where's my camera?" she asked. "I know I brought it."

"It was on the backseat of the car."

"I must have left it there. I'll go get it. I want to check on Kate, anyway—make sure she's okay."

George gave Nancy a thumbs-up sign. Then Nancy stepped into the brightly decorated suite, which was bustling with activity as people mingled and waiters served Mr. Goldman's guests. Nancy didn't see Kate, so she went straight down to the car to get her camera, then hurried back up to the suite.

As she stepped out of the elevator into the third-floor hall, she surprised someone in a black nylon wind suit and a baseball cap pulled low over frizzy black curls who was listening at the door of Mr. Goldman's suite. The person turned away and began running. The movement was so quick that Nancy couldn't tell whether it was a man or a woman.

The person shot down the hall and scurried

around the corner to the stairwell. Nancy followed. She could hear footsteps a floor below as she circled the first landing. When she got to the main floor, the exit door swept shut with a whoosh.

Nancy walked slowly down the last few steps, her eyes on the door. She crept up to it and peeked through the window at the hallway beyond. There were hundreds of people moving around—going to and from their seats and lining up at concession stands.

Suddenly, she heard a rustle of nylon and felt a hard thump in her back as someone slammed into her from behind.

"Oooomph," Nancy moaned. Someone grabbed her shoulders, then suddenly let go. Nancy heard a whoosh of the exit door. Turning around, she stumbled to the door and peered through. A few yards ahead, she saw the black nylon wind suit disappear through a door labeled Maintenance.

Catching her breath, Nancy followed and found that the door led to the dark cavelike area under the stands. Using huge limestone pillars as shields, Nancy moved farther and farther into the darkness, following the faint footsteps ahead. Finally, she peeked **around** a pillar and saw a huge wall. In front of it, the person in the black wind suit turned to face her.

Nancy ducked back behind the pillar, her heart pounding. She held her breath.

"Nancy. Nancy Drew," a voice called.

Cautiously, Nancy edged out from behind the pillar. "Who is it?" she called back. "Who are you?"

Chapter
Nine

THE PERSON STEPPED slowly forward, pulling off the baseball cap. The frizzy black curls came off with it, revealing a familiar blond receding hairline.

"Jason!" Nancy said. She did not move to greet him. In fact, she stayed on the alert, ready to run toward the crowd behind the stands. She wasn't sure she could trust Jason.

"You don't have to be afraid of me," Jason said.

Nancy rubbed her lower back. "Are you sure? You just mowed me down in the stairwell."

"I'm not going to hurt you. I'm the one who's been hurt," he whined.

"What happened? Why did you disappear?"

"I didn't disappear," he said angrily. "I was kidnapped."

"By whom? Why?"

"I don't know," Jason answered. "Two men grabbed me when I left Kate's loft Thursday night. They wore masks the whole time, and they wouldn't tell me why or who ordered it."

"How did you get away?"

"One of the kidnappers went out for food, and the other fell asleep. I was able to wriggle out of the ropes. I hitched a ride on a semi and came right here. I wanted to find Kate. Can you take me to her?"

Nancy told Jason about the phone call that Kate had received about his murder, then asked, "Have you been to the police?"

"No! I can't talk to them. Those kidnappers will kill me if I do. I know they will. They've already told everybody I'm dead."

Nancy reached into her pocket, and Jason jumped. "What are you doing?" he cried out.

"Relax. I just want to show you something." Nancy pulled out the photo that Jack had given her and a penlight. "Take a look at this. Did you see this person behind the trophy pedestal?"

Nancy watched Jason's face. He squinted, then blinked several times. His face suddenly became ashen. Without looking at Nancy, he said, "No, I don't know who it is." He glanced around quickly. "I've got to get out of here."

Jason was becoming more agitated and frantic by the moment. "Jason," Nancy said, "you have to go to the authorities. They'll protect you while they find your abductors."

"No! Absolutely not!" His face crumpled, and he rubbed his brow furiously.

"Okay, okay, just calm down." Nancy placed a hand lightly on his arm, trying to soothe him. "If you just escaped, you probably haven't heard what happened to Kate."

"Kate?" he exclaimed. "What are you talking about? She's okay, isn't she?"

"Well, not exactly," Nancy said. "Do you know anything about jewels being smuggled?"

"Jewels? No."

Nancy told Jason about Kate's arrest. "Do you think she did it?"

"I don't know," Jason said nervously. "I don't know anything about it. All I know is I've got to get away from here."

"But where will you go?" Nancy asked. "Kate's worried about you. I know she'd want to help."

"No way," Jason declared. "She's got her own problems now. If the cops and the press find out about me, it'll make things worse for her. Don't tell her you've seen me. Don't tell anyone."

"Okay, okay." Nancy thought for a minute. There was something funny about the fact that

Jason had come to see Kate but then decided he didn't want to see her at all. The photo seemed to have set him off. Also, Nancy wondered why he didn't want to report his kidnapping to the police. Was he lying about the kidnapping? Was he the one who called Kate? But if he didn't, then who did? And why? Nancy didn't want to lose track of Jason until she got answers to these questions.

"I have some friends who will help you lie low while you decide what to do," she said. "Stay over there in that corner. I'll be back in a few minutes."

"How do I know I can trust you?" Jason asked, panicky. "Why would you want to help me?"

"I'm all you've got right now," Nancy said. "Look. I like Kate, and you mean a lot to her. You can trust me, Jason."

"Okay, but don't tell anyone else I'm here!"

"I'll be right back," Nancy said, skirting the subject. "Don't leave."

Nancy ran back up to the suite. George greeted her at the door.

"Robbie made it!" she whooped. "He qualified. Sixth place. He's on the outside of the second row. Isn't that great? Hey—where have you been all this time?"

Nancy pulled George out into the hall and

closed the door. "I'm happy for Robbie," she said. "Now, listen—I need your help."

"What's up? You look like you've seen a ghost," George said.

"I have—Jason Randell." Quickly, Nancy told George about her encounter. "I'm going down to Robbie's pit to ask the Hardys to help. I don't suppose you'd like to come with me," she added with a grin.

George answered with her own broad smile.

The two girls jogged downstairs to the area under the stands. The corner where Jason was supposed to be waiting was empty. "I left him right here," Nancy murmured to George. "Jason," she said in a loud whisper. "Jason, where are you?"

After a long silence, Jason, with his wig and cap back on, stepped from behind a pillar. "I'm over here."

After introducing Jason to George, Nancy said, "Come on," and led them to the stands in front of Robbie's pit.

A high chain-link fence separated the drivers' pits from the pedestrian walkway in front of the stands. A steady stream of spectators walked along the fence, eager to be as close as possible to the drivers and other celebrities hanging out in the pits.

"George, would you mind going over to the fence by Robbie's pit?" Nancy said. "Tell Frank or Joe I need to meet one of them right away at Gasoline Alley."

Within minutes, George was back at the entrance to the stands, giving Nancy a thumbs-up. She then gestured that she was going back—to talk to Robbie, Nancy guessed.

Nancy talked privately to Frank at the Alley, briefly filling him in. "I don't want Jason to leave town," she added. "And there aren't any rooms to rent within twenty miles. Can you help? If we provide him a little cover and protection, he just might talk."

"No problem," Frank said. "There's an empty bed in the room next to ours at the motel. Doug, the crew member in that room, won't mind. He's never there—he has friends in town. I'll just tell him a friend of mine needs a place to stay."

"Perfect," Nancy said. "Just don't let Jason know you're aware of his identity."

"I won't," Frank assured her. "I can take Jason over right now. Give me a minute to get the key from Doug."

Nancy waited until Frank returned to introduce the two. "Frank, this is my friend . . . uh . . . Randy," she said. She turned to Jason, saying, "Frank's going to fix you up. Stay out of sight till I get back to you."

Nancy went to join George and congratulate Robbie. As she walked past a newspaper stand, she was startled by the headline in the afternoon paper: "Second Jewel Smuggling Suspected."

Skimming the article, Nancy learned that a major jewel heist—a million dollars' worth—had been reported in Europe. Authorities suspected the gems had been smuggled into the United States, and local police planned to question Kate Cordova.

When Frank returned to the track, Sandy and Joe were in the garage, tuning up the backup car.

"You know you could have been killed in this thing," Sandy said to Joe.

"I know, I know," Joe said, rolling his eyes at his brother. "And it looks like I'll never hear the end of it."

"Grab a wrench, Frank," Sandy said. "Give us a hand. Yes, sir, I read about your stunt in the Chicago papers," he continued from under the car. "But I don't blame you, kid. It was the kind of prank that had Robbie written all over it."

"We sure missed having you around earlier," Frank said casually. "Joe's accident wouldn't have happened if you'd been here."

"You're right there, buddy. He never would have gotten in the car in the first place."

"I've never been to Chicago," Frank said. "What's it like?"

"It's a great town," Sandy said. "One of my favorites."

Sandy slid out from under the race car. "Well, it looks like we're in pretty good shape here. I'm going back to the pit." He took a pipe from his pocket, lit it, and tossed the matches onto a small table.

"Not so fast, MacDonnell." Giovanni Randisi filled the garage door with his massive body. He wore the neon green and white jumpsuit of Jean-Claude Rochefort's crew. The sun backlit his wavy blue-black hair.

"What do you want, Randisi?" Sandy acted bored with the visitor. He slowly pulled off his gloves without meeting Randisi's gaze.

"My money, that's what," Randisi said. "You still owe me two weeks' wages."

"I owe you nothing. I carried you longer than I should have. Now get out!"

"You lead an extremely dangerous life, MacDonnell," Randisi said in a low voice. Then he stormed off.

Sandy took another puff of his pipe and tapped it out in an ashtray. "I've got to go," he said, nodding at the Hardys as he left the garage.

"Whoa. Remind me not to mess with that Randisi character," Joe said.

"He didn't seem to intimidate Sandy, though," Frank pointed out. He walked over to the little table where Sandy's warm pipe lay in the ashtray. "Look at this." He held up the dark green matchbook Sandy had used.

"'The Scotsman's Club,'" Joe read off the matchbook, "'Fourteen fifty-two Maplehurst, Chicago. Sandy must have gone there last week."

"Seems reasonable. Maybe someone at the club can give us a clue about what Sandy was doing. I think I'll give the place a call."

"You don't think Sandy is behind all the sabotage, do you?" Joe asked.

"No," Frank answered. "Why would he want to endanger his own brother? They seem really close."

"I'm hungry," Joe said, changing the subject. "Why don't I get some burgers?"

"Great," Frank said. Joe left to go to the concession stand, and Frank dialed the number of the Scotsman's Club. The man who answered told him that it was a private club and dodged Frank's other questions.

Frank hung up, then decided to check under the backup race car to make sure that it really was in good shape. Frank couldn't shake the idea that Sandy was hiding something.

A minute after Frank scooted under the car, he heard the garage door open. Man, am I hungry, he thought. "It's about time," he called out to Joe. "I hope you got plenty."

Frank heard footsteps in the garage, but his brother didn't answer.

"Joe?" he called out. "Joe!"

It was stonily quiet in the room—even the footsteps had stopped. Frank had a sinking feeling. Breathing heavily, he started to slide out from under the car.

"Who's there?" he called loudly. He was sure he could hear someone breathing. "Who is it?"

Then he heard another noise—a click. It was vaguely familiar, but he couldn't place it until the car above him began to move. His heart stopped when he realized what the noise had been.

Someone had tripped the pneumatic jack, and the car was being lowered. Frank scrambled to get out from under it, but he wasn't moving fast enough. He braced his hands on the floor and tried to push himself out from under the car. He had to save himself from being crushed.

Chapter

Ten

FRANK WAS ALMOST OUT. His head, shoulders, and torso were clear; just his legs now. Before he could pull them free, one of the huge tires slammed down, pinning his foot to the garage floor. Pain shot through his leg, and he felt as if his foot had been caught in a vise.

No matter how he struggled and squirmed, he couldn't free himself. He twisted around to see who had tripped the jack. The person ran out the door, but not before Frank saw the leg of a neon green and white jumpsuit—the uniform of Jean-Claude Rochefort's crew.

Frank lay pinned to the floor. The pain was so intense that he was afraid he might pass out.

At last Joe returned with burgers, fries, and

sodas. "Frank! What happened?" he cried out, dropping the bags. Joe raced over to his brother and started up the jack.

"Another visit from the Rochefort team," Frank said, wincing as his foot was freed.

"Randisi?"

"I don't know," Frank told him. "I only saw his leg as it went out the door. Ooh, man, that hurts."

"Come on, I'll help you to the track hospital." Putting an arm around his brother's waist, Joe supported Frank as he limped outdoors. Joe eased Frank onto a golf cart, then drove him to the track hospital.

Frank was relieved to see the state-of-the-art triage, emergency, and diagnostic facility. *Makes sense,* he reasoned—*after all, we're at a race track.* The trauma team x-rayed Frank's foot, then Frank and Joe waited for the results in the small cubicle where he'd been examined.

"Well, there are no broken bones," the doctor said when he returned, "but you do have a serious bruise." The doctor wrapped Frank's badly swollen foot with an elastic bandage as he talked. "You need to stay off your foot for a few days—you can use these crutches. Applying heat will help with the pain. If you're not feeling better by Tuesday, come back to see me."

Frank thanked the doctor, and Joe drove

himself and Frank back to Robbie's pit. "My foot can be an excuse for a trip to Chicago to the Scotsman's Club," Frank said as they rode. "I'd like to check out that place, and I'll bet Duncan Brandon could get us in," he added.

The Hardys told Robbie, Sandy, and the rest of the crew about what had happened to Frank.

"So you didn't check the lock on the jack?" Sandy said. "Pretty careless—and stupid. What's with you, anyway? Have you got some kind of death wish?"

The first day of qualifications ended with the thirty-three-car field more than half filled. Robbie's spot—in sixth—was the highest position for a rookie so far. Jean-Claude Rochefort was sitting in the outside of the third row, directly behind Robbie.

As the crew cleaned up the car, Frank talked to Sandy. "Joe and I called our parents, and they have an old friend who's a doctor. They want him to take a look at my foot tomorrow, if that's okay."

"Sure, why not," Sandy said. "Our main car is qualified, and you're pretty much out of commission for a few days anyway."

"Joe will have to go along," Frank added. "I can't drive."

"Yeah, yeah, okay," Sandy said impatiently. "We can handle the backup without him."

"We'll be back Monday morning sharp," Frank said.

By Sunday morning Frank's foot was already showing signs of improvement. It wasn't nearly as swollen as it had been the day before. After breakfast Frank called Nancy to let her know that he and Joe were making a day trip to Chicago and to ask her and George to a concert. "There's a rock concert out at Eagle Lake tomorrow night. Would you and George like to meet us there? I'll see if Robbie wants to go, too."

"Sounds great," Nancy said. "We'll be there."

The Hardys drove the four hours to Chicago, heading straight to the Scotsman's Club, an elegant eleven-story building of carved limestone.

An awning led from the curb to the entrance. "I'm glad we wore blazers and slacks," Joe murmured. "We will get in, right?"

"Mr. Brandon said he'd fix it."

A man sat behind a wooden desk at the top of a short flight of stairs inside the foyer. Frank hopped up the stairs with the aid of his crutches. "Frank and Joe Hardy," he announced. "I believe Duncan Brandon called about us."

"Ah, yes," the man said. "Welcome. You've never been here?"

"That's right," Frank said.

"The dining room is through the Grand Lounge. If you'd care for something lighter, you might try the Grille, in the far corner. There are game rooms and a library upstairs and a fitness center on the lower level. If we can be of further help, please call on me or any member of our staff."

"How about some food?" Joe asked, heading through the elegant Grand Lounge to the Grille.

"Sounds good," Frank said, maneuvering his crutches carefully across the marble floor with its thick carpets.

Over soup and sandwiches, Frank and Joe talked about the case. "It definitely looks like someone's onto us," Joe said quietly. "First the sniper at the race—"

"We don't know that for sure," Frank cut in.

"And then someone drops a car on you."

"That we know for sure," Frank said. "And he—or she, I guess—was wearing the silks of the Rochefort team."

"Giovanni Randisi," Joe said.

"Maybe," Frank answered thoughtfully. "He and Sandy had just argued before it happened.

Maybe he thought it was Sandy under the car. He couldn't really see me."

"If it was Randisi, he may not be acting alone. He may be carrying out orders from Rochefort."

When the waiter brought their desserts, Joe struck up a conversation with him about the Bulls.

After several minutes of swapping basketball stories, Frank interrupted, saying, "We hoped to run into a friend of ours here—Sandy MacDonnell from Edinburgh. Do you happen to know whether he's here?"

"I know Mr. MacDonnell. He stayed with us this past week, as a matter of fact, but I believe he went down to the Indianapolis 500."

"My brother has recently taken up Indy racing. It's a shame we missed Sandy. He suggested that we come to the Scotsman's Club—said he'd show us around the place. What do you think he'd recommend we do while we're here?"

"I'm sure he'd have you join the games on the third floor," the waiter said as he refilled their water glasses.

"Any particular one that's his favorite?" Frank asked.

"I think you'll find them all amusing," the waiter answered with a smile, "but Mr. MacDonnell especially enjoys billiards."

The Hardys finished their meal and went up to the game rooms on the third floor. It was a honeycomb of medium-size rooms connected by carved-arch openings. Each room was set up for particular games—bridge and baccarat in one, chess in another, gin rummy and poker in a third.

The farthest room was equipped with two antique billiards tables. Joe picked up a couple of sodas from the bar in the chess room and followed Frank, who was hobbling back to the billiards room. While Joe racked the balls, Frank chalked a cue.

"Maybe I can help you," a deep voice with a thick Scottish brogue said. "It's a bit awkward with two crutches and a cue, isn't it?"

A short, stocky man came from the far end of the room where he had been writing at a desk. He was bald except for a thin fringe of gray hair orbiting his pink head. Another fringe formed a half-moon enclosing the chin of his equally pink face.

"I'm Edward Bruce," he said as he chalked Frank's cue.

Frank introduced Joe and himself to Mr. Bruce. "Why don't you take on Joe?" he suggested. "I'm still a little unsteady."

Mr. Bruce kept up a steady conversation with the Hardys as he and Joe played, asking about them and telling a little about himself. "My manufacturing keeps me traveling between Chicago and Glasgow," he explained. "I miss Glasgow when I'm here, and this crazy city when I am there."

"We know people from Scotland—Robbie and Sandy MacDonnell and Duncan Brandon," Joe said as he set up the billiard balls in the wooden frame. "We're here as Mr. Brandon's guests, as a matter of fact."

"I don't really know Robbie, but I saw Sandy here just last week. We had an interesting meeting. And Duncan is an old friend. Do you share his interests?"

"Which ones do you mean?" Frank said as Joe banked a beautiful shot.

"In the games, young chap," Mr. Bruce said cryptically. "The games."

"Billiards?" Frank asked.

"Too slow," Mr. Bruce said. "Duncan's taste runs to games that involve speed."

"Oh, you mean racing," Joe said. "The Indy racing team."

"You have been teasing me, haven't you?" Mr. Bruce said with a slight smile. "We all know why you are here, especially if Duncan sent you. You are eager to join in our wagers abroad in the homeland, are you not?"

"Sure," Frank said casually. He decided to go

along with the conversation, although he wasn't sure where it was leading.

Mr. Bruce stepped back while Joe made his shot, then continued talking as he took his turn. "If you are a friend of Duncan's, I assume you're also interested in the Indy 500? And, specifically, in the young lad MacDonnell? The bookmakers in Scotland are, too—very interested. There's a whole pool putting money on him—and on others."

Joe flashed Frank a look, then Frank said casually, "Mr. Brandon told me he had great hopes for Robbie this year."

"Great hopes, indeed," Mr. Bruce said with a broad grin. "I'm sure he's told you that he has wagered a significant part of his fortune on the brash young Scot. It's his largest wager ever. And he has quite a reputation back home for wagering. I myself have placed my wager on Jean-Claude Rochefort, another promising rookie."

"How about Sandy MacDonnell?" Joe said, aiming his next shot. "You mentioned an interesting meeting with him. Does that mean he shares Mr. Brandon's interest in the Scottish pool?"

"Let's just say that for a novice, he was quite daring," Mr. Bruce said, mistakenly sinking the eight ball in the side pocket. "If you're interested, just look me up here. I shall instruct you on how to enter the pool in Glasgow." With a wink, he put up his cue and sauntered off.

The Hardys spent the next few hours nosing around but didn't discover anything more. When they finally got back to the van, Frank stretched out on the backseat and rested his foot on his sports bag. "So Duncan has bet a bunch of his fortune on Robbie," he said, looking out the window at the clear night sky. "No wonder he's anxious to stop the sabotage."

"Mr. Bruce said he and Sandy had had an interesting meeting," Joe reminded his brother. "Do you suppose Sandy was up here to place bets also?"

"Could be," Frank said as Joe maneuvered the van out of the parking garage and into the busy streets of Chicago.

"We may have a problem," Joe said after a half-dozen blocks. In the rearview mirror, he watched a black sport-utility vehicle trailing him.

"What do you mean?" Frank asked.

"I think there's a sport-ute following us. Whenever another car gets between us, he goes around it to catch up."

Frank could see the vehicle about twenty yards back, but he couldn't see the driver behind the smoked-glass windshield. He winced as he moved his foot, remembering the assault. "Lose him, Joe," he said, his jaw tight.

"Right." Joe turned the van quickly, darting down a wide alley. Left, left again, then right. He steered the van around corners, pushing the speed to the limit in an attempt to shake their dogged pursuer. Sports bags and magazines flew around inside the van as Joe zigzagged through traffic.

Skillfully, he put more and more cars between the van and the sport-utility vehicle. After a few miles, the street was clear behind them.

"Where are we?" Joe asked, throwing the map back to Frank. "Can you tell?"

Frank scanned the map with his penlight. "Looks like we're near the lake." He glanced out the window. Up ahead was a wide, dark expanse with no lights. "Look, there it is." A few Lake Michigan barges skimmed slowly over the black and choppy water.

"I think we lost him," Joe said, pulling the van to a stop on a deserted street in front of a long row of waterfront warehouses. It was dark—the only streetlight was broken. "You okay?"

"No major complaints," Frank replied. "That was some ride. Your Indy track experience is showing."

"Yeah, yeah," Joe quipped. "Well, I got the job done, didn't I?"

Just as Frank was about to answer, he was jolted out of his seat and sent sprawling on the van floor. Something had slammed into the rear of the van like a ton of bricks.

Chapter

Eleven

WHOA! WHAT WAS—" Frank started to yell as he hoisted himself back onto the seat.

Before Joe could answer, another bone-rattling jolt bounced the van.

"Somebody's ramming us," Joe said, checking the rearview mirror. "It's that sport-ute—he's trying to crush us. Hold on."

Joe started the car but the other vehicle butted the van once more before Joe could pull away. Then the sport-utility peeled away down a dark alley.

Joe tore after it. After several blocks, the other vehicle raced onto the expressway. Joe tried to keep it in his sights but lost it in the traffic.

"I got the license number," Frank said, writing it down. Joe pulled off at the next exit to check the damage.

The right corner of the back end was banged up pretty badly, but the lights were okay, and the rear and side doors still worked.

"Let's head back to Indy," Frank said. "You have to be rested for the pit stop competition tomorrow. You know the whole team competes. It will be bad enough for the crew to have me on the sick list—they can't afford to lose you, too."

"I can't believe we're spending Sunday afternoon at the art museum while they're still qualifying," George complained.

"Is it quals you're interested in or a certain redheaded driver?" Nancy teased. "Hey, if the shoot goes well, you may be in national magazine ads for Be a Sport!"

"Good point," George said with a smile.

Once the estate for a wealthy industrialist, the acres surrounding the art museum included an orchard, formal gardens, a picturesque walk along the canal, a party house, and several mansions that had been converted into historical museums.

Kate had designed a fashion shoot for her new line that would pair the models with the various sculptures sprinkled around the spacious grounds. On the spur of the moment, she had hired Nancy and George to be models for the day.

"Okay, everybody, let's make this easy on ourselves, shall we?" Kate suggested as she and Jack Herman began setting up the shot. "Goddesses, we're ready for you."

Nancy, George, and Darcy Lane, dressed in red, yellow, and blue bathing suits, took their places around the edge of a large circular pool filled with water lilies. In the center of the pool was a fountain of three Greek goddesses holding a large marble globe over their heads.

"Where's Miranda?" Nancy asked Darcy as she bounced a green- and white-striped beach ball toward George.

"In the trailer," Darcy said. "Pouting, I expect."

"What's the matter with Her Highness this time?" George asked.

"She's still upset that her agency is dropping her," Darcy said.

"Surely she'll be picked up by another agency, though," Nancy said. "She's a huge star."

"She's still pretty big in Europe," Darcy said, striking the pose Jack requested. "But Americans are getting tired of her. All those tabloid stories about her and her boyfriends—some of those guys were bad."

The girls were instructed to relax while Jack changed his light filter. "What do you mean, bad?" Nancy asked as the three took a seat on a nearby bench.

"Some were a lot older and into gambling or get-rich-quick schemes," Darcy answered. "One French guy talked her into doing some pretty stupid things. She's already been sued by people who lost a lot of money on a land deal that she lent her name to. And I hear they won't be the only ones."

"I know Jason doesn't like her," Nancy said.

"They hate each other," Darcy said. That was the second time Nancy had heard those words used to describe Jason and Miranda's relationship.

"Miranda tries to play the big shot," Darcy continued. "And you just don't do that with Jason. He really puts her down. When she got back from Florence, she found out her agency was dropping her. She blamed Jason, and they had a huge fight about it."

"I wonder if Jason is really dead," Nancy said.

"I hope not—I like him. He's the only person I know who can keep her in line." Darcy tossed the beach ball high in the air, then giggled. "Maybe the teen queen hired a hit man." Then she looked at Nancy, her dark brown eyes wide. "Don't tell her I said that, okay?"

After a few more shots around the reflecting pool, Nancy and George changed into safari pants and jackets and joined two other models at a larger-than-life bronze lion in the Shakespeare garden.

The afternoon wore on. Nancy and George had a few minutes of fun posing in Kate's clothes, mixed with hours of waiting. At times the waiting was punctuated by Kate's fits of temper and quarreling with Jack.

"I knew I'd rather be at the track," George said with a groan. "All this waiting is downright boring." The models were assembled near the *LOVE* sculpture. Created by Robert Indiana, it was his internationally famous design—*L-O* over *V-E,* with the *O* slanted to the right.

The original sculpture was enormous—twelve feet high and twelve feet wide. Kate and Jack had designed a shot that used all the models in, around, and atop the four letters. Miranda would be sitting in the *L.*

"Kate's sure in a foul mood today," George commented.

"It hasn't been the best week of her life," Nancy said. "The question is, is she upset because she's worried about Jason, because she's been falsely accused, or because she's a jewel smuggler with a questionable future?"

"Where's Miranda?" Kate yelled. "Where is she? We're ready for Miranda."

"Interesting what Darcy had to say about Miss Marott, wasn't it, Nan?"

"Very," Nancy said, checking her lipstick. "And not really so farfetched. Remember what Miranda said at Kate's loft party?"

"You mean about the trophy accident and how she was sorry you saved Jason?"

"Exactly," George said. "Maybe she wasn't kidding. I need to get to know her a little better to see what I can find out."

"If someone doesn't get our prima donna now, I'm shutting down this shoot!" Kate screeched. "Where is she?"

"She won't come out, Miss Cordova," the hairstylist said. "She has a headache."

"So do I," Kate snarled. "Its name is Miranda."

Nancy jumped up. "I'll check on her, Kate."

"Fine," Kate said. "Do it. None of my regular people have had any luck—give it a try."

Nancy walked quickly to the pink-and-orange trailer, knocked on the door, and opened it a crack. "Miranda? It's Nancy Drew. May I come in?"

Miranda was talking angrily on her cellular phone, but she motioned Nancy in.

"Don't give me that!" the young superstar yelled. "I took a lot of chances for you—I deserve some payback for them, and I want it now." She glanced at Nancy, then continued her conversation in French. Nancy understood enough to realize she was talking to a man.

After a few minutes, Miranda wound up the conversation, then threw the phone against the wall. Her face was flushed, and she was panting when she finally turned to Nancy.

"What do you want?" she snapped. Before Nancy could answer, Miranda continued, her voice calmer. "Never mind, I know. Kate asked you to get me."

She plopped ungracefully into an easy chair. She was dressed in blue shorts and a soft denim halter top. "So she's sending in the temps now," she said.

"Actually, I volunteered." Nancy also smiled as she remembered what Kate had said. "I'm a little starstruck, I guess. You've had an amazing career—how do you do it without getting burnt out?"

"Do you have a boyfriend, Nancy?" Miranda asked, glancing at the broken phone. Standing up, she took two bottles of sparkling water from the refrigerator.

"Yes," Nancy said.

Miranda nodded and flashed an understanding smile. She offered Nancy some water.

"How about you?" Nancy asked, taking the bottle that Miranda handed her.

"Right now I'm between men," Miranda said, sitting back down in the easy chair. She sighed. "I'd like to meet someone."

"I know a guy who would be perfect for you," Nancy told her.

"Is he exciting?" Miranda asked doubtfully. "I like my men to be very exciting."

"I'd say so," Nancy said. "Did you hear about the mechanic who disguised himself as Robbie MacDonnell and took a race car out onto the track?"

Miranda nodded. "Sure. I saw it on the tube that night."

"That's the guy. His name is Joe Hardy."

"He's a mechanic?" Miranda asked.

"Not really. He's from the East Coast and is working on Robbie's crew for some excitement."

"Is he cute?" Miranda asked, arching one brow.

"Sure is," Nancy said with a grin. "Blond, blue eyes, in great shape."

"Sounds like my kind of guy," Miranda said. "When and where do I meet him?"

"How about tomorrow night?" Nancy suggested. "There's a big concert out at Eagle Lake."

"I'll do it," Miranda said, standing. "I could use some new friends. All my old ones are deserting me."

"Great," Nancy said, beaming. "George and I will pick you up. We're meeting Joe and his brother and Robbie MacDonnell at the concert."

"Do you know where I'm staying?" Miranda asked. "Since this is a two-week shoot, Kate has rented a mansion on the north side for us to stay in." She wrote the address on a slip of paper and handed it to Nancy.

Nancy stood up, and Miranda laid an arm on Nancy's shoulder, leading her to the trailer door. "Well, let's get today's work over with. The sooner we do, the sooner we can start to party."

While the shot was being set up, Nancy told George about her session with Miranda.

"So who do you suppose she was talking to in French?" George wondered. "The boyfriend with the bad land deal?"

As Nancy sat in the *E* of the *LOVE* sculpture, her mind clicked away. The leather broker from Florence whom Kate had mentioned was also French, she remembered. Could Miranda have been setting up another shipment of leather bags for smuggling jewels when Nancy interrupted her on the phone? Nancy wasn't sure, but she resolved to pay close attention to Miranda.

Monday morning was cloudy and humid. Even so, there was a record turnout for the pit stop competition.

Nearly all the driving teams had entered this

traditional Indy 500 event. Two crews competed at a time, and each one would execute a typical standard pit stop by changing all four tires and simulating filling the car with fuel.

Teams would be eliminated until only the two teams with the fastest pit times were left.

"Okay, guys, the winning team splits forty thousand dollars," Sandy told his crew assembled inside the garage. "Plus bragging rights for the rest of the month. I say let's go for it—put the other teams to shame."

"What's the record?" Joe asked.

"The record was set by Danny Sullivan's team in 1985—11.742 seconds for changing four tires and fueling," Sandy answered. "Can we beat it?"

The crew stacked hands and yelled a thunderous "Bran-*don*." Then they all moved out to the track for the competition.

Frank perched on the pit wall to cheer on the team.

Jay Ronald and two other mechanics handled the fueling simulation while Joe and the other crew members made the tire changes.

After an hour of competing, Team Brandon had clocked the fastest time. As more teams were eliminated, Team Brandon became better, turning in a time of thirteen seconds, four full seconds under the next-fastest team.

"We're going to do it," Joe said, sitting down

next to Frank as they waited for their next time up. "Is Jean-Claude Rochefort's team still in? I'd love to meet them in the finals."

"That'd be pretty rare—two rookie teams in the finals. I'd sure like to go up against Randisi one on one, though," Frank said.

By the semifinals, Team Brandon was the only rookie crew left. The tire changing went without a hitch. Joe switched on the pump of simulated fuel while Sandy wrestled with the hose. Suddenly, a burst of liquid shot out from a break in the hose, drenching the crew members standing nearby.

Precious time was lost as mechanics rushed for towels or began stripping off their jumpsuits. "Don't panic," Sandy shouted. "It's simulated fuel."

"No! No!" someone screamed, whirling by. "It's real! I'm burning!"

Chapter

Twelve

H<small>ELP ME</small>!" the mechanic screamed as he spun around, his arms high in the air. Joe knew that methanol flames were invisible but still hot and lethal. The mechanic's yells were echoed by the screams from the stands and nearby pits as the spectators and other racing teams realized what was happening.

Joe grabbed a tarp and wrapped it around the burning mechanic. Then he threw him to the ground and rolled him over several times.

Robbie unstrapped himself and scrambled out of the racing pod. The Speedway fire crew arrived in seconds and doused everyone with fire-extinguishing foam.

The safety crew and paramedics hurried up. They quickly hooked up the wounded mechanic to an IV, lifted him onto a stretcher, and rushed him to the helicopter to take him to the burn center. Other crew members were checked, but everyone else seemed to be all right.

"Okay!" Sandy yelled, stomping around the pit. "Who was the idiot who grabbed real fuel instead of the simulated fuel? Hardy? Was it you?"

Joe checked the pump. "I did give you the simulated fuel, boss. Look."

Sandy checked the pump—it was clearly marked as simulated fuel for the pit competition. He sniffed the hose where it had broken. "This is real fuel," he said, his face red with fury. "It's been mislabeled. Somebody's in big trouble."

Quietly, the crew packed up and prepared to push the car back to the garage. Their run at the competition was over.

"The hose must have been cut," Joe told Frank. "This stuff doesn't tear or break by itself. It's rocket science technology."

Frank held Joe back as the rest of the crew left for Gasoline Alley. "Let's look around a little," he said.

Track officials checked the pumps while Joe searched the ground around the pit. Frank stood by the officials to hear what they were saying. Within minutes Sandy returned. The flush of his face was darker than the color of his hair.

"What are you going to do about this?" he yelled at one of the track officials. "Who gave us real fuel instead of simulated?"

"A full investigation will be launched immediately," one official said.

"It had better be," Sandy roared. "And you keep me posted!"

"What caused the fire?" Joe asked Sandy after the officials had left.

"A spark from the engine, probably," Sandy said. "It happens sometimes during a race. But it should never happen during the pit stop competition."

Sandy stormed off. Frank caught a glimpse of something wedged behind the foot of the pump. It was pointed down and looked like a small green cylinder. He tried to retrieve it, but it was jammed halfway through the grate of a spill-off drain leading to a waste runoff under the track.

Frank jiggled the end but lost his grasp. The cylinder was freed and fell through the grate to a ledge about a yard down.

"Joe, come here a minute," Frank called. "What do you think this is?" He flashed a penlight down through the grate. "It was wedged behind the pump, and when I tried to get it, I knocked it through."

"It might be some kind of holder—maybe for a cigar," Joe said. "Look—something's written on it."

Frank moved the penlight beam. "It's a letter," he said. "It's in a fancy script, and it's pretty worn, but it looks like it might be a *G.*"

"For Giovanni? As in Giovanni Randisi?"

"Maybe we can find a groundsperson or maintenance guy to get it for us," Frank suggested.

"Wait, Frank—the grate screws off with these lugs." Joe glanced around. "The pit competition is over—the spectators have pretty much cleared out. There's nobody in the pits on either side. I'll get a wrench—we can get it ourselves. If anyone questions us, we'll just say it's ours and we dropped it down the grate."

As Joe started for the garage, Nancy and George ran up. "That was a close call," Nancy said. "We saw the whole thing. What happened?"

"Frank will fill you in," Joe said. "I'll be right back."

Nancy and George ran to the pit fence and called Frank over. He told them about the fuel mixup, the cut hose, and the item under the grate.

"I hope the mechanic will be okay," George said, shaking her head.

"By the way, how's Jason?" Nancy asked. "Is he keeping pretty close to the motel?"

"Seems to be." Frank shrugged. "He comes and goes, but he never stays away too long."

While they waited for Joe, they discussed their plans for the rock concert that night at Eagle Lake.

"We'll have to meet you there," Frank said. "Robbie and the crew have to appear at the pit stop awards presentation, but we'll leave as soon as we can and head out to the lake. Robbie's coming with us—he decided to come when he found out you'd be there, George."

"Great!" George said.

Nancy and George said goodbye to Frank, then Nancy added, "Tell Joe we're returning the favor and bringing Miranda Marott just for him."

After the girls had gone, one of Robbie's crew members jogged up to Frank. "You've got a long-distance phone call, Hardy," he said. "Take it at the courtesy phone on the ramp leading to Gasoline Alley."

Frank limped out of Pit Row, went down the ramp, and picked up the receiver. The operator told him it was an overseas call and asked him to hold. Frank waited for five minutes, then the

operator returned to tell him to wait a little
longer.

Another ten minutes passed. Finally, a
thought nagged at him—his gut told him there
was something funny about this call. He hung
up and hobbled quickly back up the ramp to Pit
Row. Joe was running toward him from
Robbie's pit.

"It's gone," he said, leading Frank back to the
grate. "I got hung up talking to Sandy. When I
came back, you were gone, and this is what I
found."

Frank peered behind the pump. The grate
was resting loosely over the opening, the lug
nuts lying next to it. Frank flashed his penlight
through the grate. No green cylinder.

"Someone saw us prowling around here and
came and got it," Joe said.

"Probably the same someone who had me
pulled away with a phony overseas call," Frank
growled. "I wonder what that green thing was."

The humidity was gone, and it was a clear,
breezy night. Nancy's blue sweater and white
jeans were perfect for the weather. She and
George drove first to the north side to pick up
Miranda.

By the time Nancy, George, and Miranda
arrived at Eagle Lake, a sprinkling of stars

served as a glittering backdrop for the sailboats gliding across the glassy water.

A huge stage stretched between two massive piers, and the advance crew was setting up as Nancy staked out a perfect high, grassy spot. George helped her spread the quilts that Kate had lent them, and by the time the picnic was laid out, the Hardys and Robbie had arrived.

Robbie dropped to his knees next to George and wrapped an arm around her shoulders. "I have a present for you," he said with a playful smile. He reached into his pocket and pulled out two passes for the track garage area—one for George and one for Nancy.

"All right!" George said, giving him a big hug.

Frank opened the cooler of iced sodas and handed Nancy a tin of homemade shortbread cookies that Robbie had brought from Scotland.

"You're the mechanic who took the race car around the track, aren't you?" Miranda asked Joe. Her black pants showed off her long legs, and a green T perfectly matched her emerald eyes. "That took a lot of guts," she purred. "I like that in a man."

"Today he saved the crewman whose jump-suit caught fire during the pit stop competition," Robbie said, winking at George.

"Ooh," Miranda cooed. "A daredevil *and* a hero. This just gets better and better." She sidled over to Joe and planted herself close to him.

"How's the man who was burned?" Nancy asked.

"He's going to be fine," Frank said. "Most of the burns were superficial, and he should be out of the hospital in a few days."

"That's great," George said.

"Sandy and I think the whole thing was sabotage," Robbie told them. "Rochefort's sworn to do whatever it takes to ruin us, and it sure helps him to have Randisi on his crew. That traitor knows so much about our operation."

Nancy exchanged looks with Frank.

"The rumor around the track is that Rochefort's team has big money problems," Robbie continued. "They say that if he doesn't do well here, he won't have a ride for the rest of the season."

"Hey, Miranda, over here!"

"Miranda, give me a big smile."

Robbie was interrupted by a swarm of reporters and photographers who had spotted Miranda.

"Hey, everybody, it's going to be a great night," Miranda said, turning toward the cameras. Joe started to move away, but she grabbed his arm and pulled him back.

"Anything to say to your fans?" one reporter asked.

"I'm having a wonderful time here with Kate Cordova and her fabulous new line of teen sports clothes," Miranda said. "It's especially exciting to be here during the Indy 500. I want you all to meet the new man in my life. His name is Joe Harvey, and I'm hoping to talk Kate into using him as a model. Isn't he gorgeous, girls?"

Joe was clearly embarrassed. It was one of the few times Nancy had ever seen him blush.

"It's Hardy," Robbie said. "Joe Hardy."

"How about you, Robbie?" one of the reporters asked. "Things got pretty scary in your pit today. Is everything going to be cool by race day?"

"What happened today was—" Robbie began.

"Come on, Joe," Miranda cut in loudly. "Let's get some shots over by that boat." Miranda pulled Joe over to a beached catamaran. The reporters and photographers followed.

"What's a rookie driver compared to a superstar model?" Robbie grumbled with a reluctant smile.

"She really knows how to manipulate the press," George agreed.

"I'm going for more ice," Frank said. "Join me, Nancy?"

"Sure. You two don't mind, I take it?"

George looked down, but Robbie grinned, saying, "Not at all—take your time."

The opening act—a soft-rock male group— was just beginning its set as Frank and Nancy hiked to the concession stand.

"I don't really need ice," Frank said. "I just wanted to talk to you." He told her about someone taking the green cylinder under the grate before it could be retrieved. He also filled her in on the Chicago trip.

Then Nancy told Frank her suspicions about Miranda. "If Miranda is really having money problems, she would have a motive to smuggle jewels."

"And she had the opportunity," Frank said. "You said she was in Florence in April, and that's where the bags came from. It's hard to believe she could pull it off by herself, though. She had to be working with someone. Jason, maybe?"

"No, they don't get along. But here's another thought. Did you hear Robbie say that Rochefort's team is in trouble financially? If Mr. Goldman is having money problems, that would hurt Kate's business, too," Nancy pointed out. "Could Kate and Goldman be smuggling partners? In any case, I'm almost positive they're more than just business partners."

"You think they're romantically involved?"

Nancy nodded. "I like Kate, and I sure want to believe her, but if Goldman is in trouble, they might have pulled off the jewel heist to get ready cash."

"Then Goldman could have ordered the sabotage of Team Brandon to guarantee a Rochefort win on race day. Which means—" Frank flashed Nancy a grin.

"Our cases are connected," Nancy finished.

Frank nodded. "It makes sense. I mean, we're talking millions of dollars for the winning team."

"And Miranda could have been their connection in Florence," Nancy reasoned. "Although it's hard to imagine Kate and Miranda working together. They don't seem to get along. But then again, maybe that's why they've been at each other's throat lately."

Nancy shuddered when she thought of the dangers they had all met so far—and that Kate might be behind them. "Ask Joe to get close to Miranda to see what he can find out," Nancy said.

When Frank and Nancy got back to their picnic spot, Joe had returned, but Miranda was still holding court with the press. She didn't return until the colored lights announced the appearance of the featured rock group.

The concert was a total hit, and when it was over, Nancy, George, and Miranda made plans with the Hardys and Robbie to meet at the street festival the next afternoon.

"You'll have to be my cheering section," Robbie said. "I've been asked to participate in the caber toss at the Scottish games—and I plan to take the gold medal."

"What's a caber?" George asked.

"You'll see," Robbie called out as he hopped into the Hardys' van. "Just be there—I'm dedicating my toss to you."

"You definitely have an admirer," Miranda said to George as Nancy drove the Mustang away from the lake.

"Too bad Kate couldn't come tonight," Nancy said innocently. "Did she have other plans?"

"She was going to fit some of the models with their parade outfits," Miranda said. "In fact, she was going to our house to do them."

"Looks like they're still working," George said as they turned onto Miranda's street. "Look at the house—every light is on."

As she drove closer, Nancy had an uneasy feeling that something was wrong. Instinctively, she slowed the car. A quick movement behind the house caught her eye. It looked as if someone had plunged through the thick hedge behind the back lawn and run into the woods.

Nancy eased the car farther into the drive. Suddenly, a scream pierced the quiet of the cool May night.

Chapter

Thirteen

Nancy, George, and Miranda rushed into the house. Kate was in the living room on a couch, hysterical, the models trying to comfort her.

"What is it?" Nancy asked. "What happened?"

Kate tried to speak, but only sobs came out. She lay back as a girl laid a cool, wet cloth on her forehead.

"Kate was back in one of the bedrooms," Darcy explained. "She said she turned around and saw Jason's face in the window."

"It was pale and just hovered there, staring at her," another model added. "He was trying to communicate from the grave, I just know it.

132

Maybe he was trying to tell her who killed him."

Nancy replayed in her mind the man running from the house. It could have been Jason—same build and height. She flashed a warning look at George. She knew her old friend would follow her lead and not mention that Jason was still alive.

Kate took a few shuddery gasps, then quieted and sat up. "Nancy, I'm not crazy," she said. "I know I saw Jason's face. What do you suppose it means?"

"It probably means that you've been through a lot lately and you're stressed," Nancy pointed out. "Or maybe some other guy was peeking in the bedroom window, someone who just looked like Jason."

The tension in Kate's face relaxed a little as she took two more deep breaths. "We can drive you back to your loft," Nancy offered.

Kate shook her head vigorously. "No, I was just shocked, that's all. I'm fine now. I'll drive myself home."

Tuesday was warm and dry, a perfect day for the Indy 500 International Street Festival. A number of downtown streets, surrounding four parks, were blocked off for the event.

Dressed in jeans and Indy 500 T-shirts, Nancy and George met the Hardys at noon.

Robbie was already in the Scottish section, warming up for the games. Miranda was to meet them there in about an hour.

"You're moving a lot better," George told Frank, who had traded his crutches for a cane.

"Thanks," Frank said. "The doctor said I can get rid of the cane in a few days."

As they started up the street through the Italian section, Joe grabbed Frank's arm. "Look," he said. "It's Randisi." Turning to Nancy and George, he explained, "He's that huge dark-haired guy coming toward us."

As the Hardys turned away so they wouldn't be recognized, Joe caught a glimpse of something green sticking out of Randisi's jacket pocket.

"I knew it!" Joe said. "I knew Randisi was behind the sabotage."

"Slow down," Frank warned. "Just because he lost something around our pit doesn't mean he cut the hose. I wonder what that thing is."

"Stay here," Nancy said. "I'll be right back. Randisi doesn't know who I am."

Before anyone could say a word, she darted off, following Randisi's wavy blue-black hair. She jogged forward and saw him seat himself at a small table in front of an espresso booth.

He hung his jacket neatly on the back of his chair, the top of the green cylinder sticking out of its pocket.

Nancy bought a soda, then casually walked toward Randisi's table. When she was a few feet away, she faked a stumble and lurched forward, splashing soda on his shoulder and arm.

He leaped out of his chair as Nancy apologized profusely and handed him a small napkin. He stormed off toward the rest room behind the espresso booth.

When he was out of sight, Nancy reached into the jacket pocket behind her and pulled out the cylinder. Quickly, she went to a secluded spot behind a tree where she could still see his chair and jacket.

The cylinder was a silver case set with long pieces of jade. There was a fading ornate *G* engraved on the top. Another letter next to it was worn almost away, but Nancy could see it had been an *R*.

She pulled the case apart. Inside was a lethal-looking knife, its handle made of jade. Her pulse beat a fast rhythm in her temples. She had to get the incriminating knife and its case back before Randisi returned.

Nancy looked up to see him striding toward his table. The knife case behind her back, Nancy moved toward him.

"Oh, there you are," she said. "I was concerned. Did the soda wash out?" She avoided his eyes and looked at his damp shirt sleeve instead. The knife case felt very heavy cradled in her perspiring palm.

"Yes, it looks fine," she rattled on. "I'm sure it won't stain. I stayed here while you were gone to make sure no one stole your jacket. Oh, by the way, this was lying on the ground near your chair." She brought her hand around and opened it to show him the knife case. "Is it yours?"

He grabbed it from her with a low grunt. "Apparently so," she said with a small smile. "Well, have a nice day."

She left before he could say a word.

"Quick, let's get out of here," Nancy said as she rejoined her friends. "If he decides to follow me, I don't want him to see me with you."

They raced through the Italian and German sections, then went into the park where the Scottish games were being held. As soon as they stopped to catch their breath, Nancy told them what had happened.

"That's the final piece," Joe said. "A knife— the knife he used to cut the fuel hose."

"We don't have any solid proof," Frank said. "It's all circumstantial, but it sure makes sense."

"Now the question is," Nancy said, "is Randisi working on his own or on orders from

Jean-Claude Rochefort and/or Leon Gold-man?"

"Have I missed anything?" Miranda's pene-trating voice preceded her by half a block. "Has Robbie done his thing yet?" She lowered herself gracefully next to Joe. "Hi, honey," she said. "I dreamed about you last night."

The melodic wail of Highland pipes an-nounced the beginning of the games—caber tossing, sword dancing, and hammer throwing. Each event was held in a separate area of the park.

The games began with hammer throwing. Huge men with gigantic arms picked up sledge-hammers, twirled them around as if they were yo-yos, then flung them across the small meadow.

Sword dancing was next. Crossed swords were laid on the ground, and dancers per-formed intricate steps in the small spaces formed by the crossed sabers. Periodically, the dancers would speed up their steps and hop to another quadrant, always taking care never to touch the swords.

At last it was time for the caber toss.

"What is a caber, anyway?" Miranda asked.

"That," Frank said, pointing at what looked like a telephone pole lying on the green. "That's a peeled tree trunk—it's nineteen and a half feet long and weighs one hundred forty-one pounds. I saw this done at another Scottish festival once."

"Robbie's going to throw that thing?" George asked.

"And the one who throws it the farthest wins, right?" Miranda concluded, sounding bored.

"Nope," Frank said. "There are four judges." He pointed out one at either end of the meadow and one at each side. "The tosser has to flip the caber upside down and, at the same time, make sure it stays straight up and down in the air after it's been flipped. The judges decide which guy keeps it the most vertical after he tosses it."

"You *are* kidding, right?" George said with a grin.

"Just watch," Joe said.

There were only three caber tossers, and Robbie was last. The first man barely flipped the massive pole, and it fell over immediately. The second was a little better. After the caber flipped upside down in the air, the top was leaning over at about a twenty-degree angle.

"Whoa," Miranda gasped. "That's unbelievable."

Finally, Robbie stepped up. He was dressed in a T-shirt, the bright tartan kilt of his clan, argyle socks, and cleated shoes. He bowed to George, then took up the caber, holding the bottom of it in his palms and leaning the rest of it over his shoulder. It towered above his head. He bounced it a little as if to gauge the weight.

Nancy saw the determination that blazed across his face.

Robbie stepped up to the line, closed his eyes a moment, then opened them wide. He ran forward about twenty yards, bellowed a loud "Eeeeee-yah!" and hurled the caber. It flew through the air, then completely upended. For a moment, it hovered at a nearly perfect vertical while the spectators held their breath. Finally, the caber crashed to the ground.

An electrifying cheer burst from the crowd. Officials huddled briefly, then another cheer exploded as they proclaimed Robbie the winner.

Robbie leaped into the air, then ran to George. He reached down, pulled her to her feet, and gave her a loud kiss. The crowd cheered a third time as he picked her up, swung her around, and kissed her again.

After the games, they all headed back to the Italian section for pizza. Robbie insisted on treating to celebrate his victorious caber toss.

While he and the Hardys stood in line to pick up the orders, Miranda was waylaid by fans and began signing autographs. Nancy and George found a table with six chairs near a bubbling fountain.

As they took their seats, Nancy noticed the

man sitting at the table next to them. He was very thin, with long, graceful hands, and had the odd habit of holding his cigarette between his third and fourth fingers. Nancy was especially interested in the pinky ring he wore on his left hand—a large gold profile of Cleopatra.

"George—look at that ring," Nancy said softly, with a slight nod toward the man. "Does it look familiar?"

"The head of Cleopatra," George said under her breath. "Kate told us Silvio's leather broker wore a ring like that."

Miranda finally strolled over to the table, and Nancy asked if she knew the man with the ring.

"His name is Louis Marceau." Miranda's eyes narrowed as she looked at Nancy. "He's an importer. Why do you want to know?"

"No reason," Nancy said, shrugging. "He just reminds me of someone I used to know." Miranda seemed to lose interest in the conversation as a few more of her fans approached their table.

As Miranda talked, Marceau got up and started through the festival crowd. "Come on, George," Nancy said softly. They left the table without Miranda's noticing.

Nancy and George followed Marceau through the festival grounds and onto the downtown streets. After nearly fifteen blocks, Marceau led them through a side door into what looked like a small abandoned factory. A few windows had been broken, and the inside was littered with rusty machinery and piles of empty cartons.

Nancy and George stood near the wall. It was quiet and dark inside the building. A dim beam from a filthy skylight slashed through the dusty air. From the corner, they heard the eerie sound of small, sharp toenails clipping against the cement floor.

"Rats," Nancy said softly, shuddering.

They both jumped when a light came on in a small office across the room. Cautiously, they tiptoed across the floor. The shade was pulled down over the window in the office door.

Slowly, silently, they crept forward. When they were about a foot from the office door, they heard a silky voice from behind them. "Do not turn around. I am armed."

Chapter

Fourteen

NANCY AND GEORGE STOPPED in midstep. The silky voice behind them warned, "I am not afraid to use my weapon, so do nothing to alarm me."

Nancy noticed that the man had a heavy French accent. She couldn't see whether he really had a weapon, but she couldn't take the chance of turning to find out.

"Who hired you to follow me?" he asked.

Nancy didn't answer. There was a short silence, then the man spoke again. "Who do you work for?"

"We're just tourists," Nancy said finally. "We're in town for the race and the 500 festival activities."

"Not too much festival in here, is there?" the man said sarcastically. "I'm afraid I don't believe you."

"I can't help that," Nancy said. "We're tourists, that's all. We were wandering around downtown and thought we heard a kitten crying in here. The side door was open, so we came in. If we're trespassing on your property, we're sorry."

"If you follow me again, you will be very sorry, I assure you. Move forward. Go inside the office, but do not turn around."

Nancy and George went into the office. It was a very small room, big enough for only a desk, a chair, and a low bookcase.

The door behind them was slammed shut. They heard a scraping noise, then something thumped against the outside of the door.

It was quiet for a moment, then the light in their little room went out. They heard the man run away from the office and the building door close.

Nancy stumbled around trying to find a light switch but had no luck. "The only switch is outside the office," she said.

Nancy and George pushed against the office door, but whatever was holding it was heavy. "I'll bet he shoved one of those old machines against it," Nancy said.

"But if he could move it, why can't we?" George asked.

"He must have wedged it against the door with something else holding it. But now we've got to figure another way out of here," Nancy said, her eyes adjusting to the small amount of light. "Our only way out is through the window in the office door."

Nancy found a musty old pillow on the seat of the chair and wrapped it around her fist and arm. Turning her face away, she slammed her pillow-wrapped arm into the window in the door.

Because of the shade, only a few small pieces of glass fell inside the office—the rest splattered outside.

Carefully, Nancy and George picked the remaining shards out of the window frame. "Let me go first," George said, hoisting herself up into the opening. She sat there a moment, then reported, "You were right, Nan. He wedged a board under the wheels of a piece of machinery and jammed it in front of the door. It's going to be kind of tricky getting down."

Nancy followed George and joined her on the floor. Then they raced to the door. Once outside, they leaned against the wall, gasping and giddy at being in the late-afternoon sunlight again.

"So, are we going to tell anyone what just happened here?" George asked.

"We can tell the Hardys, but that's all,"

Nancy replied. "We don't know who else to trust yet. We can't tell the police. After all, we were following Marceau—he could say he thought we were threatening him. We never actually saw a weapon."

"But he locked us inside that office."

"In a building in which we were trespassing," Nancy pointed out. "He could say he was only detaining us while he contacted the building's owner or the police."

Nancy and George made their way back to the Scottish section of the festival. As they passed a newsstand, Nancy stopped to buy a late-edition newspaper.

"I want to see if there's any more news about that second jewel smuggling," she told George, leafing through the paper. "Here it is. The FBI says they know a second shipment left Europe for America but haven't been able to track it down in the United States yet."

By the time Nancy and George arrived back at the Scottish green, the Hardys, Robbie, and Miranda were just finishing up the pizza.

"Where were you?" Robbie jumped up and greeted George with a wagging finger. "Here I buy us a feast to celebrate my caber toss, and you duck out on the party."

"It got kind of crowded at the table with Miranda's fans, so we wandered around and got caught up in the festival and lost track of time."

Nancy could tell Frank didn't believe her by the look on his face.

After paying the check, they wandered around the festival. They had their names painted on scrolls by the Japanese Club, ate fried ice cream prepared by the Mexican Association, and wound up at an outdoor dance sponsored by the Society of Great Britain.

Nancy found a few minutes to tell Joe what had happened to her and George in the old factory. He told Nancy that he hadn't learned anything from Miranda but was working on it. Nancy asked him to find out if Miranda knew anyone with the initials B.P.

When Nancy and George finally returned to the Barbary Inn, they were too exhausted to sleep.

"I can't shake the idea that B.P. is a big clue," Nancy said, opening her laptop. She tried several stabs at passwords to open Jason's B.P. file but had no luck. "Who could it be?"

"Why don't you just ask Jason?" George asked.

"First of all, I don't want him to know we were in his flat," Nancy replied. "Second, I'm not sure whom we can trust right now." She closed her computer. "Maybe it's time to check back with the police."

* * *

Early Wednesday morning Nancy called Officer Washington. "I have a photograph you might be interested in seeing," she said. "It's from the fashion shoot the afternoon of the Speedway trophy accident. It may have a clue to what happened. There's a shadow behind the trophy. Perhaps someone was back there and the whole thing wasn't an accident after all."

"I'd like to see it, Miss Drew," Officer Washington said. "By the way, I understand your father is Carson Drew, the well-known criminal lawyer in River Heights."

"How did you find that out?" Nancy asked.

"We checked you out, Miss Drew. You kept turning up at accidents and crime scenes, and that made us curious. You have quite a reputation as a detective yourself, it seems."

"Well, I—"

"That's good enough for us. Detective Cook and I would like to come by to see the photograph you mentioned."

When the police arrived, Nancy gave them one of Jack Herman's photographs.

"Does everyone really think Kate Cordova is the jewel smuggler?" Nancy asked.

"The evidence points to her," Detective Cook drawled.

"How about the sniper?" Nancy asked. "Any clues about him—or her? We were there when it happened—"

"Naturally," Officer Washington said with a smile.

"And it looked as if the police had found the gun."

"No, they didn't," Officer Washington said. "They did find a security guard's weapon, but not the sniper's. I don't suppose you have any clues about that one, do you?"

"No, I'm afraid not," Nancy said, returning his smile, "but I'll keep in touch."

"What is going on?" Sandy MacDonnell held up a misshapen piece of metal. "It's Wednesday. The race is four days away, and I find this."

The Brandon crew had been giving their full attention to Robbie's prime car, fine-tuning it to boost its speed and efficiency.

"That's the throttle linkage," Jay Ronald said, responding to Sandy.

"It's been twisted," Joe commented, scrutinizing the metal.

"More than that," Sandy said. "Part of it has been broken off." He threw it on the floor. It bounced and spun into the corner. "Get me a backup."

Jay went to the crates stacked against the wall. He rummaged through one for a few seconds, then turned to Sandy. "They're both gone! There aren't any backups."

Sandy's blue eyes bulged with fury. Then he stormed out of the garage, slamming the door behind him.

"Where do you suppose he went?" a mechanic wondered out loud.

"Could be a lot of places," Jay said. "To Brandon's suite to beg for more money and more parts, to the river to drown himself . . . Okay, everybody, one-hour break. Robbie won't be practicing today."

Within minutes everybody had left but the Hardys.

"We've got to do something," Frank said to Joe in a low voice. "The race is Sunday, and the sabotage is getting worse."

"And this is just the stuff that we're finding out about," Joe said. "It scares me to think about some hidden problem that we won't find until it's too late."

Frank quickly stripped off his gloves and grabbed his cane. "Come on, Joe, let's go. It's time to talk to Jean-Claude Rochefort." He locked the garage door as they left.

The Hardys strode through Gasoline Alley to the Goldman team garage. Jean-Claude Rochefort was outside, signing autographs for some celebrities who were taking a special tour.

Frank waited until the driver was alone, then stopped him before he went back into his team's garage. "Jean-Claude, wait. We want to talk to you."

"Ah, no, not you—and especially not *you.*" He directed the last comment to Joe, then turned toward his garage. Joe bristled and started to respond, but Frank stopped him.

"We just want to talk, Jean-Claude," Frank said in a soothing voice. "About one of your crew members, Giovanni Randisi."

Jean-Claude whipped around. "What about him?" the driver asked.

"We think he's been sabotaging Robbie MacDonnell's car," Frank said.

"The question is, what do you know about it?" Joe added.

Jean-Claude turned to Joe, his eyes narrowing in anger. "Shut up, you amateur," he said. "I do not have to answer your questions." He turned back to Frank, saying, "Why would Randisi do such a thing?"

"Word around the track is that your team is in financial trouble. Maybe this is his way of eliminating Robbie from the competition— making it easier for you, right?"

Jean-Claude's glare turned even darker as he spoke. "That is absurd. I do not need anyone eliminated in order to do well here. I shall win on my own. Now, get out of here." He strode into his garage and slammed the door.

The Hardys walked back to Robbie's garage. Joe unlocked the door and flipped on the light. "Frank!" Joe called as he stepped over to the desk. "Get over here—quick!"

Giovanni Randisi lay lifeless on his back on the floor, the jade handle of his knife sticking out of his throat.

Chapter

Fifteen

Frank crouched to check Randisi's pulse, while Joe ran to the phone and dialed 911. Randisi was definitely dead, Frank concluded.

By the time the paramedics left with the covered body, Gasoline Alley was a madhouse. Drivers and mechanics, police and yellow-shirted guards, reporters and media people, track officials and curiosity seekers—all were swarming around the Team Brandon garage.

The police questioned everybody. They were especially interested in Sandy because he had fired Randisi.

Police officers and track security tried to hold back the press, but it was a losing battle. The murder was the first in the world-famous Gasoline Alley, and the news couldn't be stifled.

When the Hardys were finally released from questioning—with instructions to stay in town—reporters surrounded them, pumping them for more information.

By the time Frank and Joe finally escaped from the media, Robbie's garage had been taped off as a crime scene. Since they couldn't work on Robbie's cars, Frank and Joe returned to their motel room to shower and change.

"I wonder if Nancy's at the inn," Frank said. "I'm going to give her a call and tell her what happened before she sees it on the tube." He dialed Nancy's cellular phone number.

"Hi," Nancy said through the receiver. "We're just getting ready to leave. Officer Washington and Detective Cook were just here. They haven't caught the sniper yet. In fact, I don't think they have a clue who did it."

"Well, my inside information tops yours, I think. Giovanni Randisi's been murdered."

"What! How? When? Where?"

"Easy," Frank said, laughing.

"Okay, tell me everything."

Frank filled Nancy in, then added, "Joe, Robbie, and I are all suspects."

"But we thought Randisi was the saboteur," Nancy remarked.

"I still think he was," Frank said.

"Then he couldn't have been working alone," Nancy pointed out. "Whoever killed him was probably calling the shots. Randisi was just the fall guy."

Frank heard Nancy make a small sound—sort of a stifled groan. "You okay?"

"I guess so," Nancy said. "I was just thinking about how I picked up Randisi's knife. My fingerprints are all over it."

"You'd probably be a suspect, then," Frank told her, "except I overheard one of the guards say that it looked as if the knife had been wiped clean of prints."

"So what are you guys doing today?" Nancy asked. "The garage has been closed off, I'm sure."

"Right," Frank said. He paused for a moment, gathering his thoughts. "Randisi was our prime suspect. So who's really behind the sabotage? Rochefort? Goldman? They both have motives, but so do all the rest of the drivers and crews. Everybody wants to win. Maybe the key is in the gambling that we found out about in Chicago."

"You don't mean Mr. Brandon," Nancy said. "He's betting on Robbie to win."

"I know, I know."

"You mean Sandy?" she asked.

"Edward Bruce, the man we met at the Scotsman's Club in Chicago, indicated that Sandy had placed what he called a daring bet."

"But if you're saying that Sandy has something to do with the sabotage," Nancy said, "that means he bet *against* Robbie—against his own brother."

"Yeah, I know." Frank's mouth was set in a straight line. "Pretty rotten. I think I'll call my dad. He might have some contacts in Scotland who could find out something about this pool that Mr. Bruce discussed."

"We were getting ready to talk to Jason," Nancy said. "I'm stumped about this BP thing, and I know it's important. Maybe I can get him to tell us something."

"I don't think he's home," Frank said. "It's been pretty quiet over there since we've been back from Chicago. Why don't you two come on over anyway? If Jason's not back by then, we'll figure something out."

Twenty minutes later Nancy and George were greeted by Joe at the Hardys' door. "We knocked at Jason's door a little while ago. There was no answer," he said. "Here, take this extra key to his room," he continued. "Doug gave us two, and we held on to this one, just in case. By the way, I asked Miranda about B.P., and she'd never heard of him or her, either."

"Did you call your dad?" Nancy asked Frank.

"Yep. He's going to have an agent in Glasgow check on the gambling pool for us."

"If Sandy is betting against Robbie, it's going to break Robbie's heart," George said sadly.

"If Sandy was paying Randisi to be the saboteur, that may be why he stayed away for the first week," Joe pointed out. "It kept him above suspicion."

"So you figure Randisi was blackmailing Sandy?" Nancy asked.

"Could be," Frank said. "Or maybe Sandy just wanted to get him out of the way because he'd be the only witness to Sandy's part in the sabotage."

Nancy pulled a sheet of paper out of her bag and showed it to the Hardys. It was the order form labeled Accessories. "Can either of you make out any of these numbers?" she asked, pointing out the smudges.

Frank checked the paper, but had no more luck than Nancy had had trying to read the blurred numbers.

"Okay, let's try to track down Jason," Nancy said, checking the notes she had copied from Jason's appointment book. "He had a massage appointment at the sports clinic this afternoon at three. That's ten minutes from now. If he's going to come out of hiding for anything, that might be it."

The four piled into the Hardys' van and headed for the university sports center. Nancy checked with the receptionist, but Jason hadn't shown up—at least not under his real name. The four waited in the van for an hour, but there was no sign of him.

Joe called Robbie on his cellular phone and found out that the garage would be open for business again the next day. Then he called his father.

"Dad didn't get much," Joe explained. "The gambling scene in Scotland is very tight. Easy to get into but totally secure. Names and amounts are kept private. He said to check back with him later."

"Apparently they don't know about Edward Bruce," Frank said.

"Anyway," Joe said, "Dad will let us know if he finds out anything."

"So, are you guys in the parade tomorrow?" George asked.

"We're in it big-time," Frank said. "I'm driving Robbie's parade car, and Joe's riding shotgun," he said with a crooked grin. "He wanted to drive, but the track officials said no way."

"We're in the parade, too," George said. "On Kate's float."

"I thought she decided to skip the parade since she was arrested," Frank said.

"Everyone thought she should keep a low

profile for a while," Nancy said, "but she's determined to go through with it."

"Let's hope she's not making a mistake," Frank said.

Thursday morning in downtown Indianapolis was perfect for a parade. One of the highlights was the parade of drivers—thirty-three convertibles in a line, each one just like the race's official pace car. Each carried one of the race drivers perched on top of the backseat.

Frank and Joe took their places in the sixth car, and Robbie hopped onto the backseat. Frank felt his heart skip a few beats when he heard the roar go up for Robbie, one of the most popular drivers ever.

A herd of dancing horses from California followed the drivers, and after them came the first float. Kate's float was lined up halfway back between a marching band from Boston and a huge balloon depicting a cartoon cat, which was anchored by ten men holding long ropes.

Kate hurried around, giving her models last-minute clothing adjustments. It was nearly time for her float to start up.

"Okay, ladies, climb on board," Kate said. "And don't forget to strap in. I don't want anyone falling off." Her float was one of the most elaborate entries in the parade. A big sign stretched across the sides, reading Come on! Be a Sport!

Kate walked up the stepladder to the floor of the float. At the back was a small beach with real water and sand. Models in Kate Cordova originals followed her lead. Some lazed on the little beach, while others stood and waved to the crowd.

The middle of the float was a miniature mountain. Nancy, dressed in khaki cuffed safari shorts, a long-sleeved navy- and cream-striped jersey, and a black leather backpack, struck a pose halfway up. Miranda Marott, who was similarly dressed, was perched on the peak.

To show off her indoor line of teen sportswear, Kate had designed an air-conditioned clear plastic dome that was perched on the front of the float. Inside the dome, Darcy Lane, dressed in a unitard and bright pink workout skirt, would lead George and other Cordova-clad models in aerobics.

The parade began perfectly, but Miranda complained as usual. "This is higher than I thought it would be," she said a little nervously from the top of the miniature mountain.

"You are strapped in, right?" Nancy said, checking her own belt, which anchored her to the side of the mountain.

"Yeah," Miranda said. "I'm just not fond of heights, that's all—especially moving ones. Oh, well, anything for my art." She smiled broadly and waved to her fans.

Nancy looked around from her high perch. The temporary bleachers were filled with tens of thousands of people, and additional spectators hung out of high-rise windows and peered over rooftops. From her perch, she could see the thirty-three cars carrying the race drivers several blocks ahead.

Nancy glanced down at the small dome on the front of her float. "Looks like Darcy's really putting them through their paces."

"Darcy's a killer aerobicizer," Miranda said. "She'll wear them out."

As they watched George and the others doing jumping jacks, Nancy noticed a pretty blond model slow down and shake her head. Then she put her hand to her face and stopped.

"There's one who's out of shape," Miranda said.

The blond sank to her knees, her face pale. As Nancy watched in horror, another model crumpled, then another.

"George!" Nancy yelled. "George! What's happening?" It was useless. Nancy's shouts were drowned out by the music of the marching band and the cheering spectators.

Keeping her eye on the domed enclosure, Nancy frantically tried to unbuckle the strap attaching her to the miniature mountain. She watched as George raised her hand to her forehead, her face twisted. She seemed to be gasping for air.

Desperately trying to free herself, Nancy watched her friend stagger toward the front of the dome. George reached for the door but fell before she could grab it.

Chapter

Sixteen

D ARCY! LIV!" MIRANDA screamed. She pointed to the models lying on the floor inside the dome. "Somebody help them!"

As more and more spectators noticed the trouble, they began yelling and pointing. The smell of gas was so strong that it was seeping out through the plastic. A few members of the marching band ahead looked around in surprise, wrinkling their noses.

After removing her safety strap, Nancy scrambled down the mountain, a distinctive odor wafting toward her. She realized she was smelling trichloroethane, a lethal gas. The odor became stronger the closer she got to the dome.

Yanking off her backpack, Nancy raced

around to the front of the float and flung open the door to the dome. She dragged George out into the fresh air, then went back for another model.

Kate, alarmed by the cries of the spectators, finally moved to the front. She immediately called the parade officials on her remote unit and told them to have paramedics ready. Then she called her float driver, asking him to turn out of the parade at the next corner. The beach models helped Nancy drag the rest of the models out of the dome.

When the last of the aerobicizers had been rescued, Nancy closed the dome door tightly. The gas still faintly permeated the air around the dome, but fresh air filled the models' lungs, and they began to gag and cough.

Medics were waiting for the float as it left the parade. The models and George were all given oxygen, and Nancy was relieved to see the color come back into their faces.

"George, are you all right?" she asked her friend.

"What happened?" George whispered. "I'm a little woozy."

"You were gassed," Nancy said in a low voice. "Stay here and rest. I'll be right back." Nancy slipped away from the others and crept under the huge float. The float was maneuvered by a modified Jeep. The mechanical setup for the float itself—electricity, pneumatics for the ocean waves on the little beach, and stereo for the workout music—was located behind the Jeep.

Nancy followed the schematic diagram glued to the bottom of the float until she came to the unit that cooled the inside of the dome. She found three canisters of trichloroethane gas connected to the air-conditioning unit.

Nancy quickly went back to George and told her what she had found. She then informed one of the police officers at the scene.

After Kate finally finished talking to the police, she walked back over to Nancy. "What did the police say?" Nancy asked. She could see tears shimmering in Kate's eyes and a red flush coloring her cheeks.

"They blamed me," Kate said. "They said this was probably some sort of warning from a rival gang of jewel smugglers. This is a nightmare, Nancy."

Nancy reached down to pick up the backpack she had dropped and held it out to Kate.

"You can keep your outfits," Kate said to Nancy and George. "It's the least I can do."

As Nancy felt the soft richness of the fine leather, she had a sudden thought. "The backpacks really make this outfit, Kate—another of your genius strokes."

"Actually, the backpacks were Jason's idea,"

Kate said. "He really pushed them. I wasn't interested at first, but he finally talked me into them. I was right all along—they've brought me nothing but trouble."

"Because the jewels were sewn into the back-pack linings?" Nancy asked. "These were the leather bags the FBI was talking about?"

"Yes," she said with a long sigh.

"We'll see you later, Kate," Nancy said. "Try to get some rest. Come on, George."

Nancy grabbed George's arm and pulled her onto one of the small shuttles taking parade participants back to their cars.

"What is it, Nancy?" George asked when they climbed into the Mustang. "You look really excited."

"I think I figured it out, George. B.P. It's not a who, it's a what. Backpack!" She held up the leather bag. "It's definitely time to talk to Jason. Come on, I'll run you back to the inn first so you can get some rest. Then I'm heading straight for Jason's motel."

"No way," George said, shaking her head. "I'm going with you. I'm feeling better every minute, and I think we're finally onto some-thing."

With George in the passenger seat, Nancy drove back out Sixteenth Street to the motel. She parked the Mustang in front of Jason's door, then got out and knocked. There was still no answer. She placed her ear against the door.

"I don't hear anything," she said to George. There was one window in Jason's room, but heavy draperies shielded the view from outside. Nancy knocked a third time, then took out the key Joe had given her. She opened the door cautiously.

"Hello? Is anyone here?" Nancy called as the two girls stepped inside.

The room was dark and looked barely used—an odd contrast to the one in Jason's flat. The bed was made, and there were few personal things around. Nancy stepped over Jason's baseball cap on the rug just inside the door. The closet was open, and several hangers—one with a shirt still on it—were lying on the floor.

"Looks as if he might have left in a hurry," Nancy said. In the bathroom, a large towel lay wet and crumpled on the edge of the sink, and the shower was dripping.

Nancy and George checked the closet shelves and dresser drawers. They found nothing.

Nancy checked the bathroom medicine cabinet—shaving cream and razor, an unused glass tightly wrapped in cellophane, toothpaste and brush, deodorant. Then she saw a small wadded-up piece of paper in the wastebasket. She pulled it out and carefully unfolded it.

"I've got something," she announced, then

rushed over to George at the little desk and spread the paper out.

The note was in French. "'I know more jewels have entered the United States,'" Nancy translated. "'And I will not be excluded. I insist upon receiving my fair share. As you know, I am very good at arranging accidents if you try to cross me.'"

"Who wrote it?" George asked.

"It's signed with the initials L.M.," Nancy read.

"The guy with the ring?" George said.

"Right." Nancy nodded. "Louis Marceau— the man who locked us in that factory office."

"'Arranging accidents,'" Nancy repeated. "Remember Jack's photograph of the pillar in the garage area? Maybe 'arranging accidents' means pushing the trophy onto Jason."

"But this sounds as if he and Jason were working together," George said.

"Yes—on smuggling jewels. Look, there's something on the back of this note."

Two lines were scribbled in pencil on the back of the note:

KLM 702, 5p
Roch. = Gar. 11.

"It's not the same handwriting as the message on the front," Nancy said.

"What does it mean?" George asked.

"Well, the first line is probably an airline time—or even a reservation. The second—I don't know. Wait a minute. 'Roch.' might stand for Rochefort."

"Jean-Claude?"

"Right! And 'Gar. 11' could mean his garage—garage eleven at the track." Nancy stuffed the note into her jeans pocket as they hurried back to the car.

"Thank goodness Robbie gave us these Gasoline Alley passes," she said, digging hers out of her purse after they arrived at the track.

She parked a few yards from the gate to Gasoline Alley. "Here's my cellular phone," she said, handing it to George. "You stay in the car. You've had enough excitement for one day. Call KLM airlines and see if they have a flight seven-oh-two leaving at five P.M. If they do, call Officer Washington and tell him we think Marceau and Jason are the smugglers and that one or both of them might be taking that flight."

"What are you going to do?" George asked.

"Check out Jean-Claude Rochefort's garage. It seemed as if Jason was in a hurry when he left the motel—maybe he was going to garage eleven. See if you can get hold of the Hardys, too. Tell them where I am and that we may need help."

Nancy left George in the car, showed the

yellow-shirted guard her pass, and walked quickly to Rochefort's garage. There was very little action in the garage area because of the parade.

The door was open a crack when she arrived. Peering inside the windowless room, she saw the beam of a flashlight bouncing off a bag of sparkling gems in the far corner.

Nancy didn't want to let any daylight in, so she just stood there watching. Suddenly, the flashlight went out, and the dark shadow of a man with a bulging canvas bag rushed forward. The light revealed the grim, determined face of Jason Randell. She stepped back just as he shoved the door open against her.

Nancy sank to her knees, the wind knocked out of her. Gasping, she peered around the door to watch Jason disappear toward the back of the garages. She stumbled to her feet and slowly followed him.

As she moved, breathing deeply, her strength came back. She followed Jason around the fence and out the gate. He didn't seem to have a destination but was randomly moving around concession stands and among the few tourists wandering around. Once in a while, he would stop as if trying to decide what to do next.

Nancy darted in and out of the shadows to keep him from knowing he was being followed. Suddenly, he disappeared behind a door.

Nancy waited a few seconds, then followed him through the door. They were inside the Bird's Eye, a narrow five-story glass-and-chrome structure that loomed over the finish line and contained prime race-watching rooms for VIPs.

The entrance was deserted, but the elevator was going up. Nancy climbed the adjacent stairway. Through the wall, she could hear the elevator humming as it continued its climb. When she reached the fourth floor, she heard the elevator stop above her.

Hugging the wall, she crept up the final set of stairs. As she reached the top landing, she stopped to catch her breath. Nancy peered through the glass in the door that opened out onto the fifth-floor room. She couldn't see anyone, so she carefully opened the door.

Tables, chairs, banquettes, and sofas were set up for the arrival of celebrities on race day. A kitchen and bar anchored one corner. In the back of the kitchen was a door. Nancy opened it slowly and discovered a maintenance stairway with a small sign on it that read Tower Roof.

She looked around the room again. No closets, no places to hide. He must have gone up to the roof, she thought. She tiptoed up the short staircase, straining for any sounds above her.

Once upstairs, Nancy opened the roof door and looked around. No one was there. As she started back for the maintenance stairway, she heard a rustling sound beside her. Jason was charging her! Nancy stumbled with the impact.

She struggled as he dragged her across the roof, closer and closer to the edge. She reached back, clawing for something to hold on to. Jason dodged her hands, pushing her farther away.

Nancy's stomach knotted as she looked down. She could see the bricks of the race track finish line five stories below as he inched her closer and closer to the edge.

Chapter

Seventeen

H<small>ER HEART POUNDING,</small> Nancy struggled with Jason, but he grabbed her arms and held her firmly as he pushed her farther over the edge of the roof. Frantically, she looked around and spotted his duffel bag to her right.

With one daring motion, she extended her right leg and caught the strap of the canvas bag with her foot. She swung her leg around and planted her foot firmly on the edge of the roof. The strap of the bag was still around her ankle, but the bag dangled over the edge of the building.

"No!" Jason cried. "No—don't!" Nancy felt his grip on her arms relax a little as he looked at the bag.

"If you push me," Nancy said, "the bag will go, too. Think, Jason. You don't really want that to happen, do you? All your plotting, all your work—for nothing."

"Shut up. If you hadn't interfered—"

"You would be on your way out of the country, maybe?" Nancy said. "With a million dollars' worth of gems?"

The anger Nancy saw in Jason's eyes was terrifying. "How did you find out about that?" he said.

"Never mind how I found out," Nancy said evenly. "The question is, do you want those jewels splattered all over the Indy track?"

Jason let go of Nancy's arm with his right hand and reached for the bag.

Nancy quickly swung her free arm around and clipped Jason's left forearm, freeing herself from his grasp. She kicked her right foot forward, flinging the canvas bag back up onto the floor of the roof. A few sparkling rubies and diamonds tumbled out of it.

Off balance, Jason flailed his arms. Nancy could see he would fall off the roof if she didn't do something. Thinking fast, she caught his arm and gave it a firm yank. He plunged forward and tumbled onto the floor with a loud grunt.

Nancy knew she had to get away and find help. Jason had made it clear he would stop at nothing to keep from being discovered as a jewel smuggler. She raced for the roof door.

Reaching for the handle, Nancy was startled as the Hardys and George burst through the door onto the roof. Jason grabbed his bag and scrambled to his feet, but it was too late. Joe tackled him and brought him down.

"The police are on their way," George said breathlessly. "Are you okay?"

Nancy nodded and leaned against the door.

"Frank and Joe and I went to Jean-Claude's garage," George continued. "We found Randisi's locker jimmied open, but we had no idea what had happened or where you'd gone from there."

"We raced around trying to find you," Frank said. "George spotted you up here on the roof."

Nancy went over to Jason, who was slumped against the air-conditioning unit. "How could you do it?" Nancy asked him. "How could you betray Kate?"

"Hey, a million bucks is a million bucks," Jason said with a twisted smile. "Marceau and I had a pretty good deal going. I always cleared all of Kate's imported shipments, so I was able to get the jewels unpacked before she even looked at the merchandise."

"So why did you cut Marceau out of this last job?" Nancy asked.

"I didn't need him," Jason said. "When I found out that Leon was bringing Jean-Claude over for the race, and then Kate told me that we were going to shoot here, it was an ideal setup. I couldn't lose."

"The race car!" Joe said, his eyes flashing with awareness. "You smuggled the jewels in the race car!"

"I told you it was perfect," Jason said.

"Was Giovanni Randisi in on it?" Frank asked.

"Sure—I cut him in for a little. I needed a man inside Jean-Claude's crew. It was a mistake to choose him, though."

"Why?" Nancy asked. "Did he want more money? Was he blackmailing you?"

"Yeah. The pressure got to him," Jason replied. "He threatened to go to the cops if I didn't give him more."

"So you killed him," Joe concluded.

Jason's silence was answer enough.

"Did Marceau push the Indy trophy over?" Nancy asked. "Or was it Randisi?"

"It was Marceau," Jason answered. "I didn't even know he was in town then."

"Who called Kate to report that you were murdered?" Nancy asked.

"That was me," Jason said. His eyes sparkled briefly with pride. "I figured if word got out I'd been snuffed, Marceau would leave.

"I tipped off the FBI to the gems in the backpacks," Jason continued. "Thought that might scare Marceau off, too. You see, I could afford to lose those. They were nothing compared to what I'd brought over in Jean-Claude's car."

"Why did it take you so long to collect the jewels from Jean-Claude's garage?" Nancy asked. "The car's been here for a week."

"Believe me, I've been trying for days, but I couldn't get near them. Randisi was holding them hostage in his locker. Security is so tight around here, it was hard to get near the garage. When I did, Randisi was always there, protecting his interests and demanding more money. I had to get him out of the way first. And today was a good day to break into the garage because everybody was at the parade."

"I'm surprised Randisi didn't just keep all the jewels for himself," George said.

"He knew I'd kill him if he tried," Jason said with a dark look.

"You killed him anyway," Nancy said, shaking her head. She picked up the canvas bag and dropped in the two jewels that had rolled out.

"What about the sniper at the minimarathon?" Joe asked. "Did you have anything to do with that?"

"No," Jason said. He looked a little startled at the question. "Why would I?"

"One more question," Nancy asked quickly, remembering the commotion when Kate saw his "ghost" at the window. "What were you doing outside the models' house Monday evening?"

Jason's voice grew low. Perspiration beaded his brow and trickled down his left temple. "I knew Kate was out there that night. I was going to . . . to fake her suicide, so everyone would believe she was the smuggler and the case would be closed."

"You were going to kill Kate?" George said softly, her eyes wide. Jason was silent.

Officer Washington and two yellow-shirted track guards rushed onto the roof. Nancy, Frank, and Joe filled them in on what had happened, and Nancy gave them the canvas bag with the jewels.

"Looks like your reputation is well deserved, Miss Drew," Officer Washington said with admiration. "We'll make sure the FBI and Treasury know about Marceau. He'll be picked up soon, and maybe then he'll help Interpol find the jewel thieves."

Nancy, George, and the Hardys watched the men leave with Jason. "We've got to tell Kate," Nancy said sadly. "She's going to be devastated."

"Come on, Frank," Joe said. "We've probably got fifteen or twenty minutes before people hear about this. If we can, I want to check out Jean-Claude's garage again."

Frank and Joe said goodbye to Nancy and George, who left to go to Kate's loft.

Their passes got them through the gate quickly, and they rushed to Rochefort's garage. It was still empty—the door closed but unlocked. "I tripped the lock when we left earlier," Joe said, smiling.

"If they find us in here, we're dead," Frank warned in a low voice.

"They? Which they?" Joe asked.

"Jean-Claude or his crew, the police, track guards—any of them. Hurry up."

It was quiet for a few moments while the Hardys searched, their senses on high alert.

"I found something!" Joe whispered loudly from his side of the room. "Come here. Look at this!"

Frank could tell from the excitement in Joe's voice that it was something big. He ran to Joe, who was crouched on the floor next to a steamer trunk.

"Look—in the bottom drawer of the trunk," Joe said.

"Use these." Frank tossed Joe a pair of racing gloves. "So you won't disturb the fingerprints."

Wearing the gloves, Joe pulled out several rag-wrapped bundles. Carefully peeling away the cloth, he revealed the disassembled parts of a high-powered assault rifle. "Quick!" he said urgently. "Frank, give me a hand. Let's do a fingerprint test on this monster."

Frank and Joe placed the bundles in a sports bag lying on the bench. As an afterthought, Joe tossed in the racing gloves. Then they headed for the door.

"Wait a minute," Frank said. He rushed back to Randisi's locker and pulled out a wrench, holding it by the working end so he wouldn't smear any fingerprints on the handle. "Just a hunch," he told Joe as he joined him at the door.

Back at their van, Joe threw in the sports bag, then he and Frank jumped inside and locked the doors. They took out the fingerprinting kit from among the forensic investigating equipment they kept on hand in the vehicle.

First, they checked the bore of the rifle and the caliber of the bullets. "Looks like a perfect match with the ones reported in the newspaper," Frank said. "This definitely could be the minimarathon sniper's weapon."

Then they pulled fingerprints off the rifle. "Let's check these against Randisi's," Joe said. Next they checked the prints on the wrench from Giovanni Randisi's locker. Frank sighed. The prints did not match the ones on the rifle.

Frank carefully turned Jean-Claude's glove inside out and took prints off the lining. After he had eliminated Joe's prints, he compared the remaining set to those on the rifle. "Joe, look at this," he said grimly. "We've got a match."

Chapter

Eighteen

JOE LOOKED AT the two sets of fingerprints. "A match!" he repeated. "Jean-Claude's prints are on the sniper's rifle!"

"We've got to take these back to the garage," Frank said, rewrapping the bundles, "and then contact the police."

The Hardys safely replaced the rifle parts, wrench, and gloves and took their findings to police headquarters. While there, they were debriefed by the FBI about their experience on the roof.

As the Hardys were finally leaving, they ran into Jean-Claude Rochefort in the hall. He was handcuffed and being held by an officer. "I'm telling you, this is an outrage!" Jean-Claude yelled.

"You!" he shouted at the Hardys when he saw them. "This is all your doing. You framed me. I should have taken care of you when I had the chance.

"Listen to me. I've been framed," Jean-Claude insisted as they led him off. "I never saw that gun before. Someone planted it in my garage. And those guys probably did it." He pointed to the Hardys. "They work for Team Brandon. It's a perfect opportunity for them to get me out of the way so Robbie MacDonnell can win the race Sunday."

The police ushered Jean-Claude into a room and closed the door tightly, and the Hardys left the police station.

"Can you believe the nerve of that guy, accusing us of planting that assault rifle?" Joe muttered as they drove the van back to the track. "What a bozo."

"I wonder if we do have the right guy," Frank said thoughtfully.

"You're kidding, Frank. What do you mean? The evidence was all there."

"Exactly," Frank told Joe. "Maybe it was too easy. The clues were so perfect—the gloves lying right there next to the trunk where we found the rifle, for instance."

When Frank and Joe returned to the Team Brandon garage, it was deserted. While the Hardys pulled on their jumpsuits, the phone rang, and Frank answered. It was a collect call for Sandy from Chicago.

"I'll accept the charges," Frank said in a low voice, imitating Sandy's Scottish brogue.

"Sandy?" the voice on the other end of the line said.

"Yeah," Frank answered.

"Just wanted you to know that your money's down in Edinburgh—for Robbie to lose. And thanks for the tip."

The caller hung up before Frank could respond.

"What happened?" Joe asked when he saw the startled look on Frank's face. "Who was it?"

"Somebody from Chicago, verifying that Sandy's put down a bet in Scotland—against his brother."

"Against him!"

"Yep." Frank nodded.

"You know," Joe said, frowning, "with all the problems this team has gone through, Robbie has never been in danger once. Sandy could be behind the sabotage so he can cash in on his bet, but he still could be making sure that his brother doesn't get hurt. Come to think of it, the mechanic who was burned is the only person who's been hurt by the sabotage."

"You came close when you drove the race car," Frank pointed out. "Even if Randisi was behind most of it—"

"And maybe Jean-Claude—"

"Right. It sure would have helped to have someone like Sandy on the inside."

"Well, we know he's placed the bet," Joe said with a nod. "Was he just counting on the saboteurs to succeed? Or was he helping them along?"

"At the very least, he must have instructed the saboteurs not to harm Robbie," Frank mused. "But if he is an active part of it, I'll bet he's the mastermind behind the sabotage. He's not exactly the worker-bee type."

"Who are you talking about?" a voice bellowed from the garage door. "What do you mean, 'the mastermind behind the sabotage'? Who is?"

Robbie stalked into the room and over to the Hardys. Frank watched as the young driver's face flushed with anger. "Come on," he demanded. "What were you guys just talking about?"

"What everybody else is talking about," Frank said casually. "Jean-Claude getting arrested for the sniper attack. Randisi getting murdered and maybe being tied to the sabotage."

"We were wondering if they were working with someone on your crew," Joe added. "You know—someone who could have given them access to the garage."

"Randisi didn't need anyone working for him inside this garage," Robbie pointed out. "He used to work here. He had a key. He could have had an extra one made."

Robbie's bright blue eyes narrowed to a squint as he studied the Hardys. He walked over to where they stood. "Wait a minute! I thought I heard Sandy's name when I came in. Surely you're not suggesting—"

"We were just throwing out names," Joe said. "He's been acting a little mysterious . . . the trip to Chicago during the week before quals . . . just wondering, that's all."

"Are you crazy?" Robbie roared. "He's my brother. And much more than that, he's a MacDonnell. There is a sacred trust of pride and loyalty to the clan. He would do nothing to dishonor his name and the MacDonnell heritage."

"Cool it," Joe said with a thin smile. "I was just wondering."

"Get out," Robbie said, gritting his teeth.

"Both of you." His voice had become low and steely cold. "You're off this team." He started for Joe, his expression menacing. "I won't have you working for my crew. I said get out—*now!"*

Frank put his hands up to try to calm Robbie, but he could tell it wasn't going to work.

"Okay, okay," Joe said. He and Frank started for the door as Sandy and the others returned.

"The Hardy brothers have been terminated," Robbie told Sandy. "We need to find replacements right away."

No one spoke as Frank and Joe walked out of the Team Brandon garage.

"We've got to call Mr. Brandon immediately and tell him what happened," Joe said when they returned to the van. Frank took out their cellular phone and dialed the team owner, only to learn that he had been called to New York until Saturday.

Frank left word for Brandon to return their call, then called the Barbary Inn and talked to Nancy. "How did Kate take the news about Jason?" Frank asked.

"It was a real blow," Nancy answered. "But she was a little better by the time we left. Mr. Goldman was there. By the way, they're engaged—as of last night."

"At least she's completely exonerated now," Frank said. Then he told Nancy about Jean-

186

Claude's arrest and being fired from Team Brandon.

"I can't believe Jean-Claude Rochefort is the minimarathon sniper," Nancy said.

"Well, that's what the evidence says," Frank said. "How about you and George meeting us in a couple of hours for dinner at the New Rave? It's a dance club downtown. Let's do some brainstorming."

"Sounds good."

"Great. See you then." Frank clicked off, then drove back to their motel. Once there, he took out their laptop and checked their E-mail.

"There's a message from Dad," Frank told Joe. "He says to contact his agent in Edinburgh. He may have some additional information for us."

"Maybe it's about Sandy's gambling," Joe said, joining Frank at the desk. "Let's check it out."

Frank pressed a few keys and within seconds was hooked via the Internet to Scotland.

A few hours later, Nancy drove downtown and parked the Mustang in the lot behind the New Rave. The club was in a large converted warehouse. Flashing lights spotlighted the dance floor and occasionally turned on a deejay spinning CDs in a booth perched near the ceiling.

The Hardys were late. "But wait till you find out why," Joe promised.

"What is it?" Nancy asked. "More news about Jean-Claude's arrest?"

"Nope," Frank said. "We'll tell you in a minute. First, let's order. We just realized we skipped lunch."

"I'm sorry you guys got fired," George said after the waitress left with their orders for burgers, fries, and sodas. "But I don't blame Robbie for being mad. After all, you did accuse his brother. You two should understand that."

"I figured you'd defend him," Joe said, "but you should have seen him. He was steamed. He was definitely coming after me."

"Wait a minute," Nancy said. "You were going to tell us why you two were late. So, give. What's the story?"

Frank told them about the message from his father and contacting the agent in Scotland. "We found out some very interesting background about Duncan Brandon's manufacturing business."

"He had told us a little about it when he hired us," Joe said. "It has something to do with wool."

"The textile industry's very big in Scotland," Nancy said with a nod.

"Well, Mr. Brandon's really a legend there," Frank pointed out. "He's got a big textile manufacturing business, and it's all built on a machine he invented that cleans the oils and dirt out of fleece before it's spun into wool."

"This machine revolutionized the industry over there," Joe added.

"When Brandon was first starting out," Frank continued, "his chief rival was a young man named Robert Campbell."

Frank picked up a couple of fries, which had just been delivered. "Campbell had been developing a similar fleece-cleaning machine, but Brandon beat him to the patent office."

"I'm not surprised," Nancy said. "From what you've told me, I get the impression that Mr. Brandon doesn't like to lose—no matter what the contest."

"And," Joe said, "this was not the first time these two families had been rivals."

"Right, but unfortunately, it was the final blow for Robert Campbell," Frank said. "He had sunk all his money and years of his life into developing his machine. When Mr. Brandon beat him to the patent office, Campbell was ruined financially. He also saw it as a loss of clan pride. And . . ." He paused for a moment so his words would sink in.

"And?" Nancy prompted.

"He killed himself," Joe said.

"Whoa!" Nancy said.

"But what does that have to do with the MacDonnells?" George asked.

Frank took a deep breath, then said, "Robert Campbell was Robbie and Sandy's uncle."

Chapter

Nineteen

"THEIR UNCLE!" Nancy repeated. "So, you're saying that Duncan Brandon's longtime rival, a man who committed suicide because Mr. Brandon had beaten him once too often, was Sandy and Robbie's uncle?"

"Right," Frank said. "He was their mother's oldest brother."

"But we've seen how proud they are," George said. "All that family and clan loyalty. Why would they work for Brandon?"

"Big-time racing takes a ton of money," Joe pointed out. "Maybe they just felt they had to go where the money was—no matter where it took them."

"Or maybe being sponsored by Mr. Brandon was the point," Nancy offered.

"What do you mean?" George asked.

"You told us Mr. Brandon is known for being a big gambler back in Scotland," Nancy said. "Suppose Sandy gets the MacDonnells in with Team Brandon on purpose. Then he engineers the sabotage so that Robbie's cars can't run in the race."

"And Mr. Brandon loses his bets," Joe said.

"It would be a huge loss—of money *and* honor," Frank said.

Nancy nodded. "Just like with Robert Campbell."

"And Sandy makes out okay because he's betting against Robbie," Joe added.

"This is going to be so hard on Robbie," George said sadly. "His own brother, sabotaging the team and profiting from it."

"I think it's time to check in on old Sandy," Frank said, "after we finish eating."

Nancy, George, Frank, and Joe bolted their food and headed for the track. As they started to pull into Gasoline Alley, they saw Sandy's Jeep drive away.

"There he is," Joe said. "Hold on, everybody." Joe swerved the van and gunned the accelerator.

Joe followed Sandy away from the track and

onto the expressway leading to the airport. Traffic was clogged across all the lanes in both directions. Joe guided the van in and out of the lanes, always keeping Sandy's Jeep in sight.

"Do you suppose he's leaving town?" Nancy wondered.

"Could be," Frank said. "Robbie's got access to a jet. Sandy could be taking it."

The airport was bustling with travelers, and the private aviation section was especially busy because of the race. Joe skillfully maneuvered the van through the traffic to Robbie's hangar. The Jeep was parked on the side, but there was no sign of Sandy.

"Let's check it out," Frank said. The four cautiously got out of the van and walked to the small door on the side of the hangar. Frank peered in through the window and saw no one inside.

Quietly, he opened the door and led the others inside. The elegant little yellow jet sat in the middle of the large space.

"Shouldn't there be someone in here?" Nancy whispered, looking around. "It's odd that the place is deserted and unlocked."

"Maybe Sandy's on board the plane," George said.

"Don't worry," Joe said. "If we get stopped

by anyone, we won't get in trouble. Frank and I were hired by Duncan Brandon to investigate the sabotage, and that's what we're doing."

They walked over to the plane. Crouching beside the short stepstool, Frank reached up and opened the door. They all held their breath.

No sound came from the plane, so they climbed on board. Fanning out, they checked drawers and closets, looking for evidence that might prove Sandy's involvement in the sabotage.

Nancy looked out the plane's windows periodically, checking to see whether anyone had entered the hangar. "This is too easy," she murmured. "Watch it, everybody—this could be a trap."

"I think I found something," Joe called from the sleeping quarters in the tail section. The other three joined him.

"Looks like a journal of gambling records," Joe said, holding up some papers. They each took a few sheets and compared them.

On the papers were handwritten detailed records of very large bets in the name of MacDonnell—and some huge losses. The last entry was a wager against Robbie in the Indy 500.

"This proves it," George said. "Sandy has been deceiving his brother and betting against him. Poor Robbie."

"And probably sabotaging the team to guarantee that he'd win his bet," Joe added.

"Wait a minute," Frank said. He pulled out a note from his pocket. "Look."

He showed them the note. It was written by Sandy, listing work details for crew members on Team Brandon.

"The handwriting doesn't match," Nancy said, comparing the note to the gambling log. 'But look—this one does." She reached over to the dresser and picked up a publicity photo of Robbie. The handwriting on the gambling records closely resembled his autograph.

"Robbie!" Joe said. "Robbie wrote these records?"

"Then that means he knew about Sandy's gambling and maybe even the sabotage," George asked. "How could that be?"

"He's probably involved in it, George," Nancy said. She put an arm around her friend's shoulders. George was clearly upset that Robbie might have had something to do with the sabotage.

"I'm calling the police," Frank said. "I'll tell them where we are and why."

While he made the call on his cellular phone,

Nancy and Joe began putting everything back, covering up their search. George stood still, looking out the small window.

Suddenly . . . *wham!* The door to the sleeping cabin slammed shut, and they heard the lock click. They were locked in the tail of the jet!

Within seconds they heard the engines start up and felt the plane taxi out of the hangar. Frank wound up his call by telling the police that the plane was taking off.

With a slight bounce and sway from side to side, the jet left the ground a few minutes later. The four friends sat on the floor, holding on to furniture while the plane climbed into the air. Finally, they felt the jet level off, and they stood, wobbling a little.

"Okay—let's take him," Frank said. Using a credit card, he tripped the lock on the door.

They walked into the main cabin, the noise of the engines muffling their movements. Frank and Joe headed for the closed cockpit door.

"Nancy, you and George stay back," he whispered, "until we see what we've got up there."

Nancy and George crouched behind a plush leather sofa while the Hardys went to the cockpit and listened at the door. On a count of three, Joe opened the door quickly.

Nancy and George peeked over the back of the sofa. The sun from the cockpit window highlighted the pilot's head. But it wasn't Sandy's close-cropped cut—it was Robbie's wavy red hair. George gasped, and Nancy pushed her back down behind the sofa.

"Robbie!" Frank yelled.

Robbie reached out with one hand and flipped a switch. Nancy was sure he had turned on the autopilot. Then he stood and wheeled around, a shiny revolver glinting in his hand.

"I thought it was you two," Robbie said when he saw the Hardys. "I heard your voices in the sleeping cabin. So you've added breaking and entering to your many skills."

He took a step toward them. "Move," he ordered. "Back into the cabin."

The Hardys backed up, inching closer to the sofa where Nancy and George were hiding.

"We thought you were snooping into our activities," Nancy heard Robbie say. "Looks like we were right."

"We?" Joe repeated. "You and Sandy?"

"That's right," Robbie said with a proud smile. "The MacDonnell brothers. We've had a curse on our name, and at last we have an opportunity to lift it. We will let nothing—and no one—stand between us and avenging our family honor."

"Are you talking about the business rivalry

between your uncle Robert Campbell and Duncan Brandon?" Frank said.

"You two are very good," Robbie said with a nasty smile. "The Brandons have plagued our family for centuries. At last we will be able to wipe out their most prominent member. By the time this weekend is over, he will be a ruined man."

"You're going to throw the race," Joe said, shaking his head. "You're one of the best drivers out there, and you're going to take a dive so that Brandon will lose everything."

"The race is nothing compared to my family's honor."

"But people are going to suspect something," Frank said. "You're too good. You're the European champion."

"That's why we've been engineering the sabotage," Robbie said. "Everyone knows there have been problems with our car and our team. So when we fail, it won't be suspicious."

"What about Giovanni Randisi?" Joe asked. "Was he working with you?"

Robbie laughed. "No, but he was a fool and a convenient fall guy, so it was easy to implicate him—and Jean-Claude."

"How can you talk about honor?" Frank asked. "How can honor have anything to do with cheating?" He eyed Robbie's gun. "Or with murder?"

"Or burning one of your own mechanics in the fuel pump fire?" Joe added.

"Now, that was unfortunate," Robbie said. "It was purely accidental, and we were both very sorry about it. But when you're waging war, sacrifices sometimes have to be made."

Robbie rubbed his chin while he talked. "Like now, for instance. You have become our only remaining problem," he continued. "For some reason, you've been investigating our business. We've tried to discourage you, but you're very persistent. I guess I'll just have to end your snooping for good."

"Where's Sandy?" Joe asked, stalling for time. "We followed his Jeep out here."

Robbie shrugged. "He's probably taking care of business inside the airport."

From behind the sofa, Nancy looked around. A lamp cord was plugged into an outlet next to her. She took the cord in her hand and yanked hard.

A lamp jerked off a small end table and fell to the floor with a loud thump. As it fell, a shot rang out, and a bullet zinged toward the end table.

"Nancy! Watch out!" Joe yelled.

Nancy peeked over the sofa. As Robbie turned toward her, Joe jumped him. Robbie sailed backward, with Joe on top of him, and they rolled into the cockpit.

Frank headed toward Joe to help. Nancy and George leaped out from behind the sofa.

Pinning Robbie's pistol arm to the floor, Joe punched Robbie hard, but Robbie brought his other arm up and punched Joe. Joe fell back, and Robbie staggered upward. Then, leaning on the back of the pilot's seat, Robbie sent a powerful kick to Joe's midriff, sending him flying back into the cabin.

"Joe! Joe! Are you okay?" George asked, racing to his crumpled body.

"Get . . . that . . . gun!" Joe gasped, holding his midriff and moaning.

Frank raced to the cockpit as Robbie started to take aim at Joe. Frank grabbed Robbie's arm just in time and banged it a couple of times to try to dislodge the revolver.

As he wrestled with the racer, Frank twisted Robbie around so that he was between Nancy and himself. While Frank held Robbie's arm, Nancy picked up the end table and brought it crashing down on Robbie's head.

Robbie crumpled to the floor, and the gun plopped out from his fist. Frank grabbed it quickly.

Nancy dropped the end table and fell back on the sofa. As she sat catching her breath, she felt a dip, then a sudden disorientation as the plane spun sharply to the left.

Pillows and magazines flew around the cabin.

George fell hard to the floor next to Joe, and Frank slammed backward into the cockpit wall.

"There's something wrong with the plane!" Nancy yelled.

"The autopilot's off," she added. "We're going down!"

Chapter

Twenty

THE PLANE CONTINUED its sickening spin toward the ground as Nancy slid into the pilot's seat. All her training kicked in as she took control of the plane.

"Come on, baby," she said. "Let's pull you out of this." Perspiration trickled down the back of her neck, and her breath was coming in quick, shallow gasps as she reached for the controls. Outside the window, the trees around Eagle Lake seemed to be rushing up toward them.

Frank made it into the cockpit to help Nancy. "Okay, Captain," Frank said. "Let's bring her in."

Her eyes still on the controls, Nancy flashed

him a relieved smile, then barked out a few directions.

"Come on, you guys," Joe said from the cabin with a nervous laugh. "I still want to see the race Sunday."

"Yeah, well, we're working on it," Frank yelled. "Hang on."

Nancy and Frank worked frantically at the controls as the plane fell faster and faster. "Come on, come on," Frank snarled.

Just as the tops of the trees filled the cockpit window, the nose of the plane tipped up. Nancy held her breath as she pulled the plane out of its dive and leveled off.

"Whoa, that was too close," Nancy said, taking a few deep breaths.

"Nice recovery, Captain," George called over Nancy's shoulder. "I knew you could do it."

"Good job, Co-captain," Nancy said as she and Frank high-fived each other.

"Uh, I could use a hand back here," Joe said. "Looks like the bad guy's waking up."

George went back to the cabin and ripped the cord out of the lamp. Without looking at Robbie's face, she helped tie his wrists and ankles. Then she plunked herself down on the sofa and gazed out the window.

Nancy checked the clipboard hung in the cockpit for the radio frequencies, flight number, and other information. Then she called the airport.

"Hello, Indy, this is the acting pilot of flight seven-two-two," she radioed. "We have an emergency and are coming back in. Please have police waiting."

There was no response. "Hello, Indy, this is flight seven-two-two. Come in, please." She flicked the switch several times. "The radio's gone," she said with a sigh. She looked into Frank's eyes intently. "We're on our own."

"We can do it," Frank said, his voice low but steady. He gave her an encouraging nod, then called back to Joe. "See if you can find my phone. It bounced around the sleeping cabin a few times, but it might still be okay."

Following the navigational maps, Nancy and Frank turned the plane back toward the Indianapolis airport.

Joe returned to the cockpit, his hand full of several pieces of Frank's cellular phone.

"Looks like we might not need it," Nancy said. She leaned back in her seat for a moment, thrilled to see that they were being approached by two small planes and a police helicopter.

"All right!" Frank said. "Help is here at last."

As he spoke, a bullet grazed the nose of their plane.

Nancy swerved the plane away from the other

craft. Looking down, her heart sank. Sitting in the open doorway of the helicopter was a man with police coveralls and a SWAT insignia. His high-powered assault rifle was trained on their jet.

"Why are they shooting at us?" George asked.

"They must think Robbie's flying," Nancy said, "and trying to escape. I don't know how to let them know we're trying to land."

"Joe, make a sign to put in the cockpit window. Use a marking pen if you can find one—something that will really show up."

"Lipstick's good if you can't find a pen," Nancy added. "Write 'Robbie MacDonnell prisoner. Radio disabled. Trying to land.'"

George used her lipstick to print the message on a piece of paper.

Nancy had pulled high enough to put distance between their jet and the armed helicopter. Now she headed right toward the other two planes.

"Hang on, folks," Frank said. "This could be a real close encounter."

With Frank's soothing encouragement in her ears, Nancy guided the jet so that one of the other planes was alongside Frank's window. A man in the other plane glared fiercely at them and held up an FBI badge.

Frank stuck his face in the window, making sure that the men in the other plane saw him. Then Nancy leaned over him and waved. Finally, Frank held up the sign George had written.

The agent's face relaxed a little, and he talked to the others in his plane and over his radio. Then he motioned for Nancy to follow them. Within minutes, the other craft had guided Nancy into a perfect landing.

While Nancy taxied to a full stop, the passengers of the other craft swarmed toward them, some with guns still drawn.

When the others saw that Robbie had indeed been captured, they relaxed and put their weapons away.

Two federal agents took Robbie away while Frank and Joe told the others about their harrowing flight. Nancy stole a discreet look at George and was relieved to see that she seemed to be angry, not heartbroken.

"You okay?" she asked.

"Yeah," George answered. "Just mad."

"Hey, he's not worth it."

"I'm not mad at him—I'm mad at me for being so stupid and for falling for him."

"Can you come with us, Miss Drew?" an agent asked. "We'd like to hear about your adventure."

Nancy, the Hardys, and George were taken to airport security headquarters. Over sodas, the FBI and police debriefed them for about an hour.

During the session, they learned that Sandy had already been arrested. "We picked him up in the airport for questioning after your phone call from the hangar. He caved after a while— told us the whole story."

"I have to know," Joe said. "Who was the minimarathon sniper?"

"Sandy," Detective Cook said. "Dressed like a security officer. He didn't want you snooping around anymore and decided to eliminate you. He framed Rochefort by planting part of the rifle in his locker. Rochefort picked it up and was going to report it, but he was due out on the track. Sandy stole it back when Rochefort was gone. Sandy also tripped the jack that lowered the tire on your foot, Frank."

"Dressed like a Rochefort crew member that time," Frank said, shaking his head.

"Well, you were starting to worry them," the officer said. "They knew you were looking into their activities, but they didn't know why. At one point, they even thought you were working for Rochefort."

"And the fuel pump incident?" Nancy asked.

"Intended to be just more sabotage," the FBI

agent said. "Injuring their own crew member was 'an unfortunate accident,' according to Sandy, 'but worth it in the long run.'"

"For the greater good of the MacDonnell family honor," Joe muttered.

"We had an incident in Chicago you might want to check out," Frank said. He told them about their trip to the Scotsman's Club and the vehicle that rammed their van after they left.

"We'll look into it," the FBI agent said, taking notes.

"You know, I'm still thirsty," Nancy said after finishing her soda. "I'd love a glass of water."

"We don't have any water," the airport security officer said. "We have more soda, iced tea, coffee."

"I really want water," Nancy said. "I'll get a drink from the fountain in the hall. I'll be right back."

The airport was still bustling with travelers. As Nancy leaned over the water fountain, something shiny across the hall caught her eye. It was a ring on the little finger of a man leaning casually against the wall reading a paper. The ring had the golden image of Cleopatra.

She discreetly glanced at the man. His head was shaved, and he was in sunglasses and sweat clothes, but he had the same shape and size as Louis Marceau. As he brought his other hand up to his mouth, he held a cigarette between his third and fourth fingers.

When Nancy stood back up after her drink, the man caught her glancing at him and sprinted off. He recognized me, Nancy realized. It *is* Marceau.

She took off after him, racing through the airport, dodging travelers who were dragging luggage and restless children.

She watched Marceau check his watch. Quickly, he doubled back, racing past her on the other side of the corridor.

"He's going to try to board a plane," Nancy murmured to herself. "Hey!" she yelled loudly. "Stop him—the bald man in the black sweats. Stop him!"

Dozens of people stared first at her, then at Marceau barreling through the crowd. A few tried to grab at him, but he wriggled free.

"Did he take your purse, honey?" an elderly woman said to Nancy, clutching her arm. "Happened to me once."

Nancy shook her arm free, mumbling, "No, sorry," and continued her chase.

They were nearing the airport security office, where the police and the Hardys were still talking. As she ran by a newspaper stand, Nancy grabbed a magazine. Never losing sight of Marceau, she rolled the magazine into a tube as she continued her pursuit. When she passed the security office, she flung the magazine hard at the closed door.

She could hear the door open behind her as she ran. Ahead, Marceau paused briefly at the gate of his flight, fumbling for his boarding pass.

"Nice SOS," Frank called as he, Joe, and two FBI agents ran up beside her.

"Gate eleven-A," she said, panting. "It's Marceau. He just boarded." As she watched the two federal lawmen take up her pursuit, she stopped, leaning against the wall and gasping for air.

"I'd say you're about ready for the Olympics, Nan," Frank said, grinning.

The morning of race day, Joe and Frank were working in the Team Brandon pit, back on the crew. Mr. Brandon, determined to keep his car in his first Indy 500, had hired a backup driver to take Robbie's place.

Nancy and George joined Kate and her models in Leon Goldman's elegant suite above the straightaway. Only Miranda was missing. At the special request of Jean-Claude Rochefort, she was serving as his team's lap timer, sitting in the pits with a stopwatch.

Everyone in the Goldman suite was being treated to a feast of fried chicken, salads, fresh fruit, assorted breads and cheeses, and an enormous chocolate cake.

Nancy felt her excitement mount as the powerful engines started and the cars pulled out. When the pace car pulled off a few laps later, thirty-three cars revved up and the race was under way.

Nancy and George had prime seats on the balcony looking over the track. As the caterers served them lunch and drinks, they talked over the week's events.

"I don't understand how Duncan could have trusted Robbie as his driver in the first place," Mr. Goldman said. "He must have been aware of the bad blood between his family and the MacDonnells."

"Apparently not. Mr. Brandon insists he's been in the dark about all of this," Nancy said. "He knew about Robert Campbell's invention, of course, but what he didn't know was that Mr. Campbell was Robbie and Sandy's uncle. In fact, he didn't even know that Mr. Campbell had committed suicide and that the MacDonnells have been blaming him for it all these years."

Nancy took a soda from the waiter. "Their rivalry over the invention and Mr. Campbell's suicide happened before Robbie and Sandy were born," she continued, "so it's reasonable that he didn't make the connection. When he decided to back Robbie, he thought he was merely financing an up-and-coming hotshot racer who happened to be a fellow Scot."

"He was definitely that," George said. "Now he'll be an up-and-coming convict."

"And Mr. Brandon won't lose everything after all, right?" Kate asked. "Even with Robbie out of the race?"

"Not everything," Nancy said. "His backup driver might not win, but Joe says he's good enough to finish in the top ten. That will still put the team in pretty good money."

"The police told me that Louis Marceau confessed that he hired a local thug to push the trophy onto Jason and that he trapped you two in the old factory," Kate said to Nancy and George. "He also connected the gas to my float—he thought I was working with Jason," she added.

"And Jean-Claude Rochefort was completely exonerated?" Mr. Goldman asked.

"Yes," Nancy answered. "He didn't have any part in the sabotage. Robbie and Sandy just made him look guilty—like when they planted Randisi's monogrammed knife holder near the fuel pump."

"Did you get a chance to ask the Hardys about that sport-utility vehicle that rammed them in Chicago?" George asked Nancy. "Do they know who did it?"

Nancy briefly told Mr. Goldman and Kate about the incident. "Frank told me that one of the waiters there owns a vehicle like the one they saw," she added. "The police found it in a body shop getting the dents hammered out, so it's probably the same one. The Hardys might have to go up and ID the fellow as the waiter they talked to earlier. Apparently he's a good friend of Sandy's and had become suspicious of the Hardys' questions."

Nancy and the other spectators in the Goldman suite sat on the edge of their seats for most of the exciting race. It was nearly a perfect afternoon—a few blown engines and a brush with the wall here and there, but no major accidents. Jean-Claude streaked to an exciting first-place finish and, from Victory Lane, dedicated his win to Miranda.

Although they had worked for an opposing team, the Hardys were welcomed to the Goldman suite after the race to join Nancy and George for a celebration. Several reporters crashed the party looking for quotes from victorious owner Leon Goldman, his fashion designer fiancée, and his guests.

"So, Kate, you've had quite a week," one reporter said. "Any thoughts to share with us?"

"Folks, I'd like to introduce you to my friends," Kate said, pushing Nancy, the Hardys, and George forward. "You can tell the world that the successful launch of Be a Sport! plus a glorious Indy 500 would never have happened without the help of Nancy Drew, Frank and Joe Hardy, and George Fayne! I'm sure they wouldn't mind answering a few questions."

"Mr. Joe Hardy," one reporter with a French accent said, "I have a question."

"I'll be happy to answer," Joe said with a friendly smile for the cameras.

"Tell us what it was like to date supermodel Miranda Marott," the reporter asked.

"I don't believe it," Joe groaned, turning back to his friends. "After all that's happened around here, that's what they're interested in."

"Well, Joe"—Nancy laughed—"that's what you get for racing with the big boys."

THE HARDY BOYS CASEFILES™

☐ #1: DEAD ON TARGET	73992-1/$3.99	
☐ #2: EVIL, INC.	73668-X/$3.99	
☐ #3: CULT OF CRIME	68726-3/$3.99	
☐ #4: THE LAZARUS PLOT	73995-6/$3.75	
☐ #8: SEE NO EVIL	73673-6/$3.50	
☐ #12: PERFECT GETAWAY	73675-2/$3.50	
☐ #14: TOO MANY TRAITORS	73677-9/$3.50	
☐ #32: BLOOD MONEY	74665-0/$3.50	
☐ #35: THE DEAD SEASON	74105-5/$3.50	
☐ #47: FLIGHT INTO DANGER	70044-8/$3.99	
☐ #49: DIRTY DEEDS	70046-4/$3.99	
☐ #53: WEB OF HORROR	73089-4/$3.99	
☐ #54: DEEP TROUBLE	73090-8/$3.99	
☐ #56: HEIGHT OF DANGER	73092-4/$3.99	
☐ #57: TERROR ON TRACK	73093-2/$3.99	
☐ #61: GRAVE DANGER	73097-5/$3.99	
☐ #65: NO MERCY	73101-7/$3.99	
☐ #66: THE PHOENIX EQUATION	73102-5/$3.99	
☐ #69: MAYHEM IN MOTION	73105-X/$3.75	
☐ #72: SCREAMERS	73108-4/$3.75	
☐ #73: BAD RAP	73109-2/$3.99	
☐ #75: NO WAY OUT	73111-4/$3.99	
☐ #76: TAGGED FOR TERROR	73112-2/$3.99	
☐ #77: SURVIVAL RUN	79461-2/$3.99	
☐ #78: THE PACIFIC CONSPIRACY	79462-0/$3.99	
☐ #79: DANGER UNLIMITED	79463-9/$3.99	
☐ #80: DEAD OF NIGHT	79464-7/$3.99	
☐ #81: SHEER TERROR	79465-5/$3.99	
☐ #82: POISONED PARADISE	79466-3/$3.99	
☐ #83: TOXIC REVENGE	79467-1/$3.99	
☐ #84: FALSE ALARM	79468-X/$3.99	
☐ #85: WINNER TAKE ALL	79469-8/$3.99	
☐ #86: VIRTUAL VILLAINY	79470-1/$3.99	
☐ #87: DEAD MAN IN DEADWOOD	79471-X/$3.99	

☐ #88: INFERNO OF FEAR	79472-8/$3.99
☐ #89: DARKNESS FALLS	79473-6/$3.99
☐ #91: HOT WHEELS	79475-2/$3.99
☐ #92: SABOTAGE AT SEA	79476-0/$3.99
☐ #93: MISSION: MAYHEM	88204-X/$3.99
☐ #94: A TASTE FOR TERROR	88205-8/$3.99
☐ #95: ILLEGAL PROCEDURE	88206-6/$3.99
☐ #96: AGAINST ALL ODDS	88207-4/$3.99
☐ #97: PURE EVIL	88208-2/$3.99
☐ #98: MURDER BY MAGIC	88209-0/$3.99
☐ #99: FRAME-UP	88210-4/$3.99
☐ #100: TRUE THRILLER	88211-2/$3.99
☐ #101: PEAK OF DANGER	88212-0/$3.99
☐ #102: WRONG SIDE OF THE LAW	88213-9/$3.99
☐ #103: CAMPAIGN OF CRIME	88214-7/$3.99
☐ #104: WILD WHEELS	88215-5/$3.99
☐ #105: LAW OF THE JUNGLE	50428-2/$3.99
☐ #106: SHOCK JOCK	50429-0/$3.99
☐ #107: FAST BREAK	50430-4/$3.99
☐ #108: BLOWN AWAY	50431-2/$3.99
☐ #109: MOMENT OF TRUTH	50432-0/$3.99
☐ #110: BAD CHEMISTRY	50433-9/$3.99
☐ #111: COMPETITIVE EDGE	50446-0/$3.99
☐ #112: CLIFF-HANGER	50453-3/$3.99
☐ #113: SKY HIGH	50454-1/$3.99
☐ #114: CLEAN SWEEP	50456-8/$3.99
☐ #115: CAVE TRAP	50462-2/$3.99
☐ #116: ACTING UP	50488-6/$3.99
☐ #117: BLOOD SPORT	56117-0/$3.99
☐ #118: THE LAST LEAP	56118-9/$3.99
☐ #119: THE EMPEROR'S SHIELD	56119-7/$3.99
☐ #120: SURVIVAL OF THE FITTEST	56120-0/$3.99
☐ #121: ABSOLUTE ZERO	56121-9/$3.99
☐ #122: RIVER RATS	56123-5/$3.99
☐ #123: HIGH-WIRE ACT	56122-7/$3.99

What's it like to be a Witch?

Sabrina
The Teenage Witch™

"I'm 16, I'm a Witch, and I still have to go to school?"

◆◆◆◆◆

#1 Sabrina, the Teenage Witch
by David Cody Weiss and Bobbi JG Weiss

#2 Showdown at the Mall
by Diana G. Gallagher

Based on the hit ABC-TV series

Look for a new title every other month.

From Archway Paperbacks
Published by Pocket Books

1345-01

Nancy Drew
on Campus™

By Carolyn Keene

- [ ] 1 New Lives, New Loves   52737-1/$3.99
- [ ] 2 On Her Own   52741-X/$3.99
- [ ] 3 Don't Look Back   52744-4/$3.99
- [ ] 4 Tell Me The Truth   52745-2/$3.99
- [ ] 5 Secret Rules   52746-0/$3.99
- [ ] 6 It's Your Move   52748-7/$3.99
- [ ] 7 False Friends   52751-7/$3.99
- [ ] 8 Getting Closer   52754-1/$3.99
- [ ] 9 Broken Promises   52757-6/$3.99
- [ ] 10 Party Weekend   52758-4/$3.99
- [ ] 11 In the Name of Love   52759-2/$3.99
- [ ] 12 Just the Two of Us   52764-9/$3.99
- [ ] 13 Campus Exposures   56802-7/$3.99
- [ ] 14 Hard to Get   56803-5/$3.99
- [ ] 15 Loving and Losing   56804-3/$3.99
- [ ] 16 Going Home   56805-1/$3.99
- [ ] 17 New Beginnings   56806-X/$3.99
- [ ] 18 Keeping Secrets   56807-8/$3.99
- [ ] 19 Love On-Line   00211-2/$3.99
- [ ] 20 Jealous Feelings   00212-0/$3.99
- [ ] 21 Love and Betrayal   00213-9/$3.99

Available from Archway Paperbacks

Simon & Schuster Mail Order
200 Old Tappan Rd., Old Tappan, N.J. 07675
Please send me the books I have checked above. I am enclosing $_____(please add $0.75 to cover the postage and handling for each order. Please add appropriate sales tax). Send check or money order--no cash or C.O.D.'s please. Allow up to six weeks for delivery. For purchase over $10.00 you may use VISA: card number, expiration date and customer signature must be included.

POCKET
B O O K S

Name _____

Address _____

City _____ State/Zip _____

VISA Card # _____ Exp.Date _____

Signature _____

1127-18